PUFFIN BOOKS

SPY DOG
SUPERBRAIN

Andrew Cope lives in the middle of England. He's lucky enough to have two pet pigs and a dog called Lara. The pigs are very clever but have never had a book written about them. 'Spy Pig' just doesn't sound right.

His dog isn't so clever. Or at least, she doesn't show it. Which got Andrew wondering whether she was just hiding it? Could Lara be undercover as a secret agent? Perhaps she's just pretending to be stupid? Maybe her sticky-up ear means she's always on alert? And besides, 'Spy Dog' sounds like a much better title.

If you would like Andrew to visit your school, please email him at andy@artofbrilliance.co.uk. He may even be able to bring Lara!

Books by Andrew Cope

Spy Dog
Spy Dog 2
Spy Dog Unleashed!
Spy Dog Superbrain

SPY DOG
SUPERBRAIN

ANDREW COPE

Illustrated by James de la Rue

PUFFIN

PUFFIN BOOKS

Published by the Penguin Group
Penguin Books Ltd, 80 Strand, London WC2R 0RL, England
Penguin Group (USA) Inc., 375 Hudson Street, New York, New York 10014, USA
Penguin Group (Canada), 90 Eglinton Avenue East, Suite 700, Toronto, Ontario, Canada M4P 2Y3
(a division of Pearson Penguin Canada Inc.)
Penguin Ireland, 25 St Stephen's Green, Dublin 2, Ireland (a division of Penguin Books Ltd)
Penguin Group (Australia), 250 Camberwell Road, Camberwell, Victoria 3124, Australia
(a division of Pearson Australia Group Pty Ltd)
Penguin Books India Pvt Ltd, 11 Community Centre, Panchsheel Park, New Delhi – 110 017, India
Penguin Group (NZ), 67 Apollo Drive, Rosedale, North Shore 0632, New Zealand
(a division of Pearson New Zealand Ltd)
Penguin Books (South Africa) (Pty) Ltd, 24 Sturdee Avenue, Rosebank, Johannesburg 2196, South Africa

Penguin Books Ltd, Registered Offices: 80 Strand, London WC2R 0RL, England

puffinbooks.com

Published 2008

5

Text copyright © Andrew Cope, 2008
Illustrations copyright © James de la Rue, 2008
All rights reserved

The moral right of the author and illustrator has been asserted

Set in Bembo
Typeset by Palimpsest Book Production Limited, Grangemouth, Stirlingshire
Made and printed in England by Clays Ltd, St Ives plc

British Library Cataloguing in Publication Data
A CIP catalogue record for this book is available from the British Library

ISBN: 978-0-141-32244-5

www.greenpenguin.co.uk

For my favourite mum and dad

Thanks to:

Will Rawling — for the ending. I knew it was right as soon as you suggested it!

My family — for allowing me endless hours sitting at a laptop when I should have been helping with homework or listening to clarinet practice!

The brilliant team at Puffin for making it all happen. Especially Sarah, Shannon, Sophie, Reetu and Jennie.

Mark, Ju, Pid, Mick, Pat, Bail and Woody — for bringing me back down to earth every Thursday night.

Jacqui Stone — for exporting the books to her rellies in Oz.

All the children who have emailed or written to me — I grin so much it hurts!

Contents

1. Royal Flush

'It's boring,' yawned Ollie. 'I mean, we've been waiting ages.'

'Shush,' hissed Mum, adjusting her hat. 'It's not boring. It's the most exciting thing that's ever happened to us. It's not every day that you get to meet the Queen.'

The Cook family waited patiently, Ollie passing the time by picking his nose. The Queen was working her way down the line, politely chatting to all the award winners. 'She's nearly here,' gasped Mum out of the side of her mouth. 'Best behaviour, everyone.'

Ben and Sophie smoothed their clothes and stood straight, tummies in, chests out. Ben quickly cupped his hand and put it to his face, checking his breath. He didn't want to breathe pickled onions on Her Majesty.

Ollie rolled his eyes and sighed. He stuck his finger up his nose and rummaged around as he watched the elderly lady gradually move closer. Before he knew it she was talking to his family, shaking their hands. Dad was actually introducing him to the Queen! Ollie did his best photograph smile and bowed, like he'd practised. Now Dad was asking him to shake hands with the Queen. 'Er, but, Dad,' he said, thinking of what was on the end of his finger.

'No "buts", mate.' Dad frowned. 'Your Majesty, I'd like you to meet our youngest, Oliver. He's only four but played an important role in capturing the villains.'

The Queen bent down and her face broke

into a warm royal smile. She took Ollie's hand and shook it. Ollie thought he saw her smile fade as she felt something sticky on the end of his finger. She quickly got out a hankie from the small bag she was carrying. Then she opened her mouth to speak, but Ollie couldn't wait to be spoken to. 'You look just like the lady on the stamps,' he beamed. The Queen opened her mouth again, but Ollie carried on. 'And I've been wondering – have you got a PlayStation? I bet you've got every game in the world,' he added. 'And have you ever had anyone's head chopped off?'

'That's a lot of questions,' said the Queen. She flashed a confused smile and turned her attention to Ollie's older brother. 'And you are . . . Benjamin,' she noted, looking at his name badge. 'Tell me about your adventures, young man.'

Ollie watched as his brother flushed bright red. He stammered a few words before Dad stepped in. 'All three of our children have been involved in catching the criminal gang, Ma'am. But the key to it all is our special dog, Lara.'

The family pet wagged her tail furiously.

She stood on her hind legs and did her very best curtsey. Her Majesty shook the dog's paw. 'I've heard a lot about you, Lara,' beamed the Queen. 'I know, for instance, that "Lara" stands for "Licensed Assault and Rescue Animal". Or should that be "GM451"? My Prime Minister has kept me informed. He tells me you are the world's first superdog. A spy, no less,' she chuckled. 'What a fantastic thing to be. My Prime Minister also says you are top secret, though.' Lara watched as the Queen swept her hand along the line of award winners. 'So all the others will get their faces in the papers, but you must remain anonymous. What a shame.' The Queen turned her attention back to Ben. 'Maybe you will get some glory one day, but I suppose Lara is like a real-life

superhero. She has to keep her identity secret. It must be jolly exciting.'

Jolly exciting indeed, agreed Lara, wagging her tail. *Just glad to be of service.*

'Yes . . . it is,' Ben replied nervously.

The head of state did her best royal smile and continued to wipe her fingers on a hankie. 'We already have 007. Does that make Lara 00K9?' chortled the Queen, proud of her joke.

The family laughed, perhaps a little too heartily, except for Ollie. 'I don't get it,' complained the youngest member of the family.

'Ah, he is not amused,' remarked the Queen, attempting another royal joke. 'Well, get this, young man. I'll make sure that you and your family have a small reward for capturing the criminal gang.'

No need, Ma'am, thought Lara. *Capturing criminals is all in a day's work and family life is the only reward I need.*

'And, of course, you must all stay for tea at the Palace,' suggested the Queen, smiling. 'My husband and I love having children in the house.'

'House,' whispered Sophie to her brother, gazing round at the suits of armour. 'She calls Buckingham Palace a "house".'

Ollie grumbled his way through the next ceremony. Trumpets sounded and the Queen rested a sword on the shoulders of some of the award winners. Ollie couldn't help noticing that they all seemed very pleased. He was hoping the sword would slip and she'd accidentally chop someone's head off. 'Or maybe just an ear,' he whispered to Mum. 'Like Henry the Eighth used to do. That would be so cool.'

Ben nudged his younger brother as Lara stepped forward. 'She's the first ever dog to receive such an honour,' he beamed as they watched the Queen tap a sword on their pet's shoulders.

'Wow,' exclaimed Ollie, suddenly taking an interest. 'And why is she doing it, anyway?'

'Lara captured those baddies and rescued the Millennium Diamond. She's a hero,' explained Mum. 'People who've done lots of good things can get knighted. That means they become "sir" somebody-or-other. You know, like "Sir Richard Branson". Or "Sir Alex Ferguson".'

Ollie mulled it over. Next in line was a lady with a huge nose. She stepped forward and the Queen touched her shoulders with a sword. 'So is she a "sir"?' asked Ollie, watching the ceremony with growing interest.

Mum listened carefully to what the Queen was saying. 'No,' she smiled. 'Men become "sirs" but ladies become "dames". Lara has just become a dame. And that lady has been rewarded because of all the brilliant work she's done at her school. She's a head teacher whose school had some of the best exam grades in the country. Imagine! What a fantastic achievement. She's really earned the honour.' Mum cast a sideways glance at her youngest son. 'You have to be a special person to become a sir or dame.'

But Mum had never been more wrong. The family smiled as the lady received her damehood from the Queen. Nobody suspected that the head teacher had an evil plan that would plunge Lara and the children into another adventure.

2. Disco Dog

There was only one day to go before the six-week school holidays. All the children were excited because Mr Bell had announced it would be a non-uniform day. Ben, Sophie and Ollie were especially thrilled because Lara had been invited to their end-of-year party. She was the guest of honour and would be giving out the awards.

'It's not very often that your pet dog gets to do this kind of thing,' Ben explained to his younger brother. 'Lara is very special,' he reminded him. 'For a start, she's received an honour from the Queen. And not all dogs can play on the PlayStation, strum the guitar and send emails, you know.' Ollie just shrugged. He wasn't bothered about Lara's damehood but he thought it was cool that his pet dog played wrestling games and helped him with his homework.

It had been an eventful few months. The adventures had all started when the Cooks had adopted Lara from the RSPCA. In fact, they hadn't adopted Lara at all; *she* had chosen *them* as part of her Secret Service mission. And Lara wasn't even her real name. She went by the code name GM451. The collar round her neck said 'LARA' in boldly engraved letters, but it actually stood for 'Licensed Assault and Rescue Animal'. She was the Secret Service's biggest achievement. The Queen had been right to describe her as a canine James Bond.

Lara and the children had soon developed a very special bond. They played, laughed and shared adventures together. The children were delighted to learn that Lara could understand them, even if she couldn't actually speak. They all loved their pet. Ollie was the youngest and he took his dog's amazing skills for granted. He was a bright, upbeat boy with a loud voice that he used to talk to anyone, any time, even if they weren't interested. So, even if Lara could have spoken, she wouldn't have got a word in edgeways with Ollie.

Sophie was much quieter and more thoughtful than her younger brother. She had smiley eyes set in a freckle-covered face. Lara spent hours with her, writing stories and drawing pictures. She was the best homework assistant ever, helping Sophie to the top of her class.

Sophie and Ollie looked to their older brother for guidance and, usually, Ben led them well. He had shot upwards recently and all his clothes were too small. Fortunately, Ben was good-looking and anything he wore suited him. He could probably be in a boy band one day if it wasn't for his terrible dancing skills.

All three loved having a pet dog, especially one that was also a secret agent. However, Lara's special status meant they'd been drawn into some serious scrapes. Things usually turned out OK in the end, but Mum had thrown a few wobblies, especially when the children had been chased by a baddie with a gun. Incredibly, it even turned out well when Lara had been shot. The good news was that it meant she wasn't fit enough to return to Secret Service work so she had been allowed to stay at the Cooks' full time. Lara had enjoyed the thrill of life as a secret agent but being a family pet was much better. It was far from boring for her, and she got plenty of thrills as well as oodles of love.

Lara's Spy Dog training had been very intensive. The Secret Service had spotted her at an early age and she'd worked one-to-one with an animal scientist, Professor Maximus Cortex. His lifelong work had been to create the world's first superanimal and he'd achieved his ambition with GM451. He and the Cooks still kept in touch, and the professor had grown very attached to Ben, Sophie and Ollie. The scientist invited Lara back to his secret spy headquarters twice a year. Officially, it was so GM451 could be updated on the latest gadgets but Lara wasn't fooled. She knew it was so the professor could see the children.

Lara loved Professor Cortex. He was old and crotchety on the outside but a big softie on the inside. She knew he would never admit it, but she thought he loved her too. Despite her soft spot for the professor, Lara's life had moved on. His world was one of spies, gadgets, adventure and danger. Her new world was one of walkies, picnics, bike rides and family fun. She had relaxed a bit. The professor's rules seemed less important since she'd retired from the Secret Service. Her world was now far less dangerous and Lara had bent the rules slightly.

The Cooks lived in a small village and most of the neighbours knew of Lara's special abilities. She acted like an old-fashioned sheriff, riding into town and sweeping crime off the streets – the good, the bad and the ugly all rolled into one. Lara had even started an animal neigh-bourhood watch – training the village pets in basic spy tactics. Occasionally she was invited into the local school to run self-defence classes and she was delighted that the local community had taken her to heart.

In return for Lara eliminating crime, the villagers had promised to keep her special status a secret. There had been some reporters snooping around a while back, but Lara had seen them off. She'd had a bit of trouble with a diamond robber but he'd ended up behind bars. Lara and the Cooks had had a quiet few months out of danger and that's how she wanted to keep it.

Lara had spent most of the day getting ready for the end-of-year party. She'd soaked in a nice warm bath and then got wrapped in her special doggie dressing gown. She chose her favourite CD and turned up the volume, wiggling her hips as she finished getting

ready. There would be a disco at the party and Lara wanted to show off some of her doggie moves. Mum had given Lara a good brush and blow-dry. She smelt lovely and looked all fluffy. She cleaned her teeth with Ben's electric toothbrush and curled her lip in the mirror, running her tongue against her sparkling white fangs. *Superb. What marvellous gnashers.* She dabbed some of Mum's perfume behind her ears and finished with a bit of Dad's hair gel, spiking up her fringe. Lara took a look in the mirror and raised an eyebrow, James Bond style. She saw a black and white dog, Labrador size, with a bullet hole in her upright ear. The diamond on her collar looked a million dollars. *Probably because it is*, she thought, before admiring her new image. *Fantastic*, she thought. *I love the fluffy look. Rather cool, if I say so myself.*

Lara let herself out of the front door and trotted to school. She arrived just as the bell went, not only signifying the end of the school day but the start of the summer holidays. Excited children poured into the hall where Lara was waiting to greet them.

She reserved her biggest, wettest licks for Ben, Sophie and Ollie.

The party went really well. Lara joined in with most of the dancing, shaking her doggie bottom and strutting her stuff to the beat. She didn't mean to show off but when she took to the floor and started doing some of the moves she'd practised earlier, everyone clapped and whistled.

'She's quite a mover,' one of Ben's mates shouted to him above the din of the music.

'And look at how brilliantly she plays the air guitar,' exclaimed another.

Ben nodded his head in agreement. Watching Lara he still couldn't believe that this was the end-of-year party and his last term at this school. It wouldn't be long before he was starting at Chellaston.

Lara was glad when the disco finished and she could grab a breather and a slurp of squash. She and the children took their seats and Mr Bell got up on stage. He did a terrific speech about how fantastic the children had been all year and then announced the winners of several end-of-year awards. Lara was

introduced as the guest of honour and leapt on to the stage to massive applause. She sat proudly, her bullet-holed ear standing to attention, shaking paws with the winners and putting medals around their necks. *What a lovely school*, thought Lara. *And the head teacher is just perfect. The kids love him and all want to do their best.* The retired spy dog stood on stage with the winners and did her best doggie smile.

'Say cheeeese,' sang the photographer.

I'd prefer sausages, Lara thought as she smiled. The flashbulbs made her blink. *What a perfect end to a perfect school year*, she beamed.

3. The Brain Game

Six smartly dressed teachers sat round the table. It was daytime but the blinds were drawn. Their meeting was top secret.

The new head teacher was a pencil-shaped lady in a floral dress. She had a sharp face and thin lips that looked incapable of smiling. Her distinguishing feature was a pointy nose, held high so she could peer down at the assembled audience. She tapped her pen on a teacup for attention. 'Welcome to the first meeting of the school year,' she announced. 'I'm so pleased to be at Chellaston School and I hope you will join me in making this institution the best in the country. I have selected you all for this special project because I know you will help me with this dream. Any questions before I proceed?'

'Not a question exactly,' came a voice from the back. 'But we'd like to congratulate you on your recent honour at the Palace. We are all very proud of you, *Dame* Payne.'

'Why, thank you, Mr Wilde.' She smiled, although secretly she thought she deserved the recognition for her genius. 'It's an honour that we can all share as we strive for the same results here. I was very successful at my previous school and I will not be seen to fail here. As I confirmed during our holiday meetings, we have secured funds from our private sponsor to pay for the world's top scientists to create an intelligence formula. Once it's ready, our formula will breed superchildren around the globe and we will be rich beyond our wildest dreams.'

'How is the formula coming along?' asked a lady on the left.

Dame Payne fiddled with her laptop and an image of a brain was beamed on to the big screen. 'We're making excellent progress,' she purred. 'It's basically ready, but our scientists need the final ingredient – the brain tissue from an intelligent child. It has to be quite young. Still growing. This "superbrain" is the key to everything.' There was silence in the room as the head teacher tapped at her laptop once more. 'Which brings me to the rules for next term. Results in this school are up across the board.' Her thin lips turned up at the corners but her eyes remained unsmiling. 'Congratulations to all members of staff concerned. But, as the new head, I'm telling you that we have to do better,' she snorted. 'And the only way to improve the school's exam results is to work the children even harder. Only then will we have the superbrain we need.'

There were murmurs of approval from the other teachers. 'Agreed,' said Mr Wilde.

'I will work them overtime in science. But we need the whole team to do the same. If we are to get our pupils' grades into the best in the country then I vote we start the new regime from September.' He eyed the other teachers, stroking his ginger beard with excitement.

'But isn't it a bit cruel?' asked Mrs Grey, the English teacher.

'Good Lord, no,' objected Dame Payne, shaking her head. 'Nooo, noo, no. It's science, Mrs Grey. It's a sacrifice in the name of the advancement of the human species. Think of this as a "donation". The DNA from the brain will go into our intelligence formula and it will revolutionize learning. I would imagine the chosen child will think it an honour to give their brain for the good of the world.'

'But the chosen child will have their brain *removed*,' continued Mrs Grey.

Dame Payne failed to hide her annoyance. 'You make it sound so . . . final, Mrs Grey. Their brain will last forever.'

Mr Wilde thumped the table in agreement. 'As a science teacher, I assure you that this is the most exciting advance in the history of humankind. And we only need one child. Can't you see how exciting this is?' he bellowed. 'Finding the perfect child is the last piece in our jigsaw. So, let's really push them this year and decide on the chosen one as soon as we can.'

'I'm in,' growled Mr Stern, a large man in a checked suit. 'Let's accelerate our plan. In my lessons there's going to be no Mr Nice Guy. I really want the chosen one to be from my class.'

'Of course you do,' soothed Dame Payne. 'What an honour that would be. So let's go through the new rules once more,' sniffed the head teacher, clicking to a summary slide.

'Rule number one: extra homework,' she read. The members of staff broke into satisfied smiles. 'Every subject, ev-er-y night. It's the only way. Work them until they drop,' she said. Her lips almost smiled. 'This has the added advantage of weeding out the skivers. They will drop out of school and you'll be left with the strongest. It's simply "survival of the fittest". Exam results are bound to go through the roof,' she noted, 'as the weaker kids are farmed out to normal wishy-washy schools where average is acceptable.'

Dame Payne's eagle eyes peered out at the teachers, waiting for their murmuring of approval to die down. Even Mrs Grey was nodding now. 'Number two: no playtime,' announced the head teacher. 'After all, it's just wasted time. There's no brain growth. Why should kids chase around the playground using up valuable energy when there's maths to be done? I mean, what possible benefit can playtime be? Consider it abolished.'

She watched the collective nods round the table and continued to point three. 'A personal favourite of mine,' she admitted. 'Earlier starts and later finishes to the school day.'

'Which, combined with Saturday school, will really accelerate brain growth,' agreed a lady from the left. 'My pupils are going to have extra Spanish and Japanese on Sundays.' She felt adoring eyes on her. 'Compulsory, of course,' she purred.

'Excellent, Miss Steele,' nodded the head.

'That's exactly in keeping with what this school is trying to achieve. After all, the superbrain won't grow by accident.'

Dame Payne advanced to the last slide in her presentation. 'And finally,' she continued, 'total control. Any child answering back, missing school, failing to do homework or complaining about the new regime is out. O. U. T. Out. No appeal. No fuss. They are expelled. That will soon sort out the whingers and get us down to those who really want to work.'

'Perfect,' grinned Mr Wilde, rubbing his beard again with glee. 'Very soon we will be in a position to decide on the chosen one. And, shortly after that, we'll have their brain in a jar and an intelligence formula that will change the world.' He stopped for a second, considering that he may also receive an honour from the Queen. '*Sir Anthony Wilde*' *has such a nice ring to it*, he thought. 'These rules are crucial to our success,' he finished.

'Any questions?' asked Dame Payne, staring over the top of her spectacles and taking in all the members of staff. 'No?

Then I challenge you to grow the best brains you can.'

Ben wasn't exactly looking forward to September. It was usual for children to be a bit nervous of the step up to the big school. If he'd known that his new head teacher would stop at nothing to secure the brain of one of the best pupils, he'd have moved from 'nervous' to 'terrified'.

Ben read the Chellaston School handbook as he sat in the kitchen with Lara and his dad. The inside cover had a 'Welcome to our school' section, written by the new head teacher. He looked at the picture and shuddered. His gaze was automatically drawn to her nose, then her lips, which were firmly pointed downwards at the corners. 'And those piercing eyes. They go right through me,' explained Ben, holding the picture up to show his dad. 'She must have chosen her best photo for this handbook. If this is Miss Payne at her best, I'd hate to see her at her worst!'

'That's "Dame Payne" to you,' chuckled Dad. 'We saw her at the Palace, remember?

You're very lucky to have a head teacher who's achieved such brilliant results.'

'But she looks so . . . cold,' said Ben, shuddering.

Dad laughed again. 'I'm sure she's a terrifically warm woman and a great head teacher,' he said. 'Looks can be deceiving. Take your dog, for example.' He smiled, casting a glance at Lara. 'Do you think she's beautiful?'

Absolutely, nodded Lara, arching her back in a doggie stretch.

'Certainly not,' said Dad. 'At least, not on the outside.'

Pardon me? Not beautiful on the outside? Lara sniffed.

'Look at her,' Dad continued. 'Does she look highly intelligent?'

Lara sat and scratched her bullet-holed ear. *Supremely clever*, she glared.

'Of course not,' said Dad, answering his own question again. 'I'm sure Lara would agree that she doesn't look beautiful or clever.'

Well, you're no oil painting yourself, she frowned. *And you're not exactly Einstein either.*

'I think she's adorable in her own way,' Ben protested.

'Let's just say, first impressions can be misleading,' insisted Dad. 'Everything will be fine. Dame Payne will turn out to be a really nice lady and you'll finish top of the year. Get your brain in gear and everything will turn out brilliantly.'

Dad was wrong on both counts. Dame Payne's passport face was hiding pure evil on the inside. Even worse, if Ben got his brain in gear it would end up in a jar.

4. Pet Shop Adventures

Ben, Sophie and Ollie were enjoying their six weeks off. The family had spent an unusually quiet few days by the coast. Mum was relieved and a little surprised to come away with just a suntan. 'We haven't solved any crimes or got into any scrapes,' she said on the way back. 'What a relief!'

The children and Lara sat in the back, sighing. 'What a boring holiday,' mouthed Ben to Lara.

She nodded and winked. *Perhaps there will be some fun when we visit the professor's new lab next week*, she thought to herself.

The next week soon arrived, and Lara and her adopted family went to visit Professor Cortex's Spy School. They looked forward to these visits because they were shown all kinds of gadgets. And the professor always went to great lengths to make sure their visit was top secret. The only thing they knew this time was that his laboratory had moved. Lara took a late-night phone call and Ben watched as she scribbled notes, using a pencil held in her mouth. She put the phone down and fetched her glasses from the lounge. Placing them on the end of her nose, she pored over a road map. Ben watched her following a line with her paw, frowning with concentration. Then she gave him a paws-up sign.

Should be OK, she thought. *I think I can get us there.*

It was an early start the following day. The Cook family piled into the people carrier, and Dad followed Lara's left and right paw signs as she looked at the map. They headed out of town and turned on to the motorway, soon arriving at the next big city. Lara directed Dad to park in an out-of-town shopping centre.

Mum looked puzzled. 'Are you sure, Lara?' she asked. 'Surely the top secret Spy School is going to be miles from anywhere. It can't be here, can it?'

If my calculations are correct, Mrs C, this is exactly where we should be, woofed Lara, undoing her seat belt and opening the van door. *Although, I agree, it does look a bit unlikely.* She looked around. There was a superstore, McDonald's, a furniture store, electrical retailer, DIY warehouse and a pet supermarket. The family piled out of the car.

Ben stretched. 'Which way, Lara? Or have we just stopped for a burger?' he asked, rubbing his belly and smacking his lips together.

Lara gave her best disapproving look before trotting confidently towards the pet superstore. The doors swished open and in she went, the family following at a distance. Lara sniffed. *Pet food*, she thought. *Yuck!* Lara had only tried dog food once, and hated it. She always ate her meals at the table with the family. She loved chilli con carne, lamb curry and bangers and mash with Mum's home-made gravy. *But my favourite has to be spag bol*, she thought, licking her lips. She sniffed again. *I can smell budgies and hamsters and — what's that? Some rabbits, I think. Doesn't smell like a top secret Spy School.* She made her way to customer services and waited for the others to catch up. While she was waiting she pressed the button on her collar and a small piece of paper fell out of the pouch. She gave it to Dad. *Go on,* she urged. *Do what it says and we're in.*

Dad looked round at everyone and smiled nervously. 'Are you sure, Lara?' he asked.

All eyes fell on the family pet, who nodded. *Go on,* she encouraged. *These are the instructions from the professor. Spies always have secret words.*

Dad approached the customer services lady and cleared his throat. 'Erm, hello,' the others heard him say. 'This may sound like a strange request, but —' Dad hesitated while he re-read the note — 'we're looking for an unusual pet.'

The customer services lady smiled at him. 'What kind of unusual?' she asked.

Dad consulted his note once more. He looked round at the family again, feeling a little stupid. *Go on,* thought Lara, *spit it out, man. This is the code that gets us in. You have to get it right.*

'Have you got any . . . zebras?' Dad blurted, ignoring Ollie's snort behind him. 'Er, yes, zebras,' repeated Dad, looking down at his note again. 'A male one,' he added. 'Black with white stripes.'

'Not a female?' asked the lady. 'Are you sure?'

Dad consulted the note one last time. 'No, they would be white with black stripes. We definitely don't want one of those,' he read stiffly.

'We might have some in stock,' said the lady matter-of-factly. 'But we keep them somewhere special. Please follow me and I'll show you.'

The customer services lady flounced to the back of the store, out of sight from prying eyes. 'Cool, we're getting a pet zebra!' exclaimed Ollie as they marched behind the lady. 'A boy one.'

The Cooks gathered at the far corner of the shop, in the exotic pets section. The customer services lady stood on tiptoes and made sure there were no more customers around. When the coast was clear she spoke quietly into her collar. 'Male zebra, alpha code correct,' Ollie heard her say. 'Roger. Twenty seconds.'

The four-year-old was a bit confused. The only 'Roger' Ollie knew was his granddad.

'Is Granddad helping choose our new zebra?' he asked.

The lady smiled. 'Please gather round and look at this exotic parrot,' she said. The Cooks all turned to see a stuffed parrot on a perch. 'It's not real,' said Sophie. 'It's a dead parrot.'

The lady smiled at Mum and Dad. 'Press the parrot's beak,' she explained. 'Quickly – we only have ten seconds left.'

Everyone looked at one another, confused. As the time ticked away, Ben moved his finger towards the stuffed parrot and held it over its beak. He looked at Lara and she nodded. *Go on then, pretty boy*, she thought. *Our seconds are nearly up.*

Ben winced as he pressed the beak. Nothing happened. He looked at Lara. 'What now?' he asked.

Suddenly there was a creaking sound as the floor below them started to drop.

Hold tight, thought Lara as the family started to plunge downwards at an alarming rate.

5. A Top-secret Secret

The Cooks all held on to each other as they plummeted down. Finally, the platform stopped and the family stepped off, watching it zoom upwards. The professor was delighted to see them, rubbing his hands together as if he was a boy scout lighting a fire. He was dressed in his usual all-white lab outfit and insisted that the family get changed into their own versions of superwhite clothes before they entered the inner sanctum of his top secret Spy School.

The Cooks emerged from the changing room looking like a family from a soap powder commercial. Lara looked fantastic in her white socks. 'We've come to collect our zebra,' piped up Ollie. 'We want a boy one, please.'

The professor looked momentarily con-fused. 'Ah yes, the code word,' he beamed. 'Sorry about all that kerfuffle but there are a lot of prying eyes. What we do here is top secret and we can't have just any old Tom, Dick or Harry stumbling on our hidey-hole now, can we?'

Lara shook her head, agreeing with him.

'Right,' said the professor. 'Let's go.'

He marched the family along a corridor and into a huge underground sports hall. They assembled round him and watched a pack of trainee spy dogs being put through their paces.

Ben peered into the weights room and nudged his sister. 'Hey, Sophie,' he urged. 'Look at that monkey on the exercise bike.'

'Fitness is the key,' barked the professor. 'All our animals need to be top-class athletes. The best in their field. Isn't that right, GM451?'

Lara remembered the assault courses she used to do so easily. *I think I may have let myself go a bit*, she winced, breathing deeply and drawing her belly in. *I must cut down on custard creams.* The dogs were organized into a game and Lara watched as they nosed a football around the hall. *I can't resist*, she thought. *Footy is my favourite thing*. Lara bounded on to the playing area and barked to the other dogs. *OK, guys, over here. Swing a cross in and I'll show you how to finish*. The ball sailed towards Lara. She leapt acrobatically and powered a volley into the top corner, past a diving Labrador goalkeeper. *Pick that out, Fido*, she whooped, sliding across the floor on her furry tummy. The children clapped enthusiastically but Professor Cortex tutted loudly.

'GM451,' he announced, 'you are not here to play the fool. We have some serious business to conduct – if you can bear to drag yourself away?'

See you guys later, woofed Lara to her new teammates. *Captain Sensible wants a word*.

The professor smiled sarcastically as Lara joined him for the guided tour of the sports hall. 'As you know, this is Spy School number two, an offshoot, because we've been so very successful. I have several exciting new gadgets to show you, GM451,' he announced. 'And one very special invention, but that can wait. Here,' he said, throwing Lara a tartan coat.

Oh no, Prof, she thought. *That's one of those silly coats that little dogs wear. You know, the ones who are really pampered by their owners. Yappy dogs. I can't wear that, it's too uncool.*

The professor continued, as if reading her mind. 'I know it may look a little silly, GM451,' he agreed. 'But this is specially designed. Get yourself strapped in tightly, if you please.'

Ben fumbled with the buckles until Lara was fitted snugly into her new tartan coat. Sophie looked at her pet and giggled. Lara stood with drooping shoulders, her bullet-holed ear at half mast. *It's not even my colour,* she thought. *Can we get this over with, please?*

Professor Cortex continued, as enthusiastic as ever, fastening a helmet to Lara's head. 'Righty-ho,' he announced. 'This coat has a grappling hook built in. Press this button here,' he said, pointing to a small remote clipped on to the coat, 'and the hook will shoot upwards.' The professor beckoned Lara over to the indoor climbing wall. 'Here,' he said, 'aim for the ledge at the top.'

Lara steadied herself before pressing the button with her paw. She heard a click and a rope shot upwards from her jacket, a small anchor latching on to the ledge above. *Hey, that's really clever.* The scientist tugged the rope to check it was safe. 'And this button here will reel you in, like a fish on the end of a line.' The professor couldn't resist pushing it for her and Lara was hauled up to the ledge at an alarming rate. She looked down on the sports hall. *Hi, everyone,* she waved, surprised but impressed with the professor's gadget. *It's like a reverse abseil. Now how do I get down again?* she wondered.

The Cooks grinned up at Lara, and Ollie waved excitedly. The professor clapped and hopped. 'Excellent, GM451. I'm afraid we haven't worked out how to get down yet, so I'll send one of my assistants for a ladder.'

The family went through to the professor's lab. Mum and Dad had a coffee and the children drank lemonade while they waited for Lara to be retrieved. Eventually the family pet slunk into the room, looking a bit upset at being left on the ledge for so long. *Will someone please remove this ridiculous coat?* she thought as she shuffled into the room. *Those trainee dogs have lost all respect for me. I can't believe you guys left me up there.*

'Sorry about that, GM451,' apologized the professor. 'But it's a very handy gadget. You must keep it. You never know when it might come in useful.' He smiled. 'Or maybe you could just wear the coat to keep you warm?' he suggested.

I'd rather freeze to death than let my mates see me in that thing, she thought, sipping her water.

'And I've got something else to show you, GM451,' announced Professor Cortex, reaching into his pocket. 'Get a load of this little beauty.' He placed what looked like a dog poo on the table. All eyes fell on Lara.

Don't look at me, she glared. *I didn't do it. I'm toilet-trained, remember?*

'It's a poo–cam,' exclaimed the scientist, hopping from one foot to the other in his excitement. He picked it up. 'Looks and feels just like dog poo. Even smells like it,' he said, twitching his nose. 'But crucially, GM451, it's fake. And it contains a very small video camera. It allows us to beam high-quality digital images from anywhere in the world.'

'Poo-cam,' echoed Dad, loving the word.

'See here,' beckoned the professor, pointing to a large flat-screen monitor. 'We have poo-cams positioned all over the world.' He clicked the remote and a picture of 10 Downing Street was projected on to the screen. 'These are live pictures,' he explained, clicking through the channels. Dad recognized the White House in Washington, Big Ben in London and the European Parliament in Brussels. 'We just place a poo-cam where we want and, hey presto, we can spy instantly. Quite perfect.' The family watched footage that showed the garden of Buckingham Palace. Mum put her hand across her mouth as one of the princes pegged out his boxer shorts. 'The Palace is easy,' explained Professor Cortex. 'They have so many corgis that our fake poo has gone completely unnoticed.'

'Very clever,' agreed Dad. 'I mean, hardly anybody's going to remove your camera, are they? Because – well – because it's disgusting, basically.'

'Oh, completely disgusting, sir,' smiled the professor, nodding enthusiastically. 'Disgustingly simple. I always think the best inventions are the simplest. And this is just brilliant.'

'Can I borrow one?' asked Ollie, thinking of all the tricks he could play.

'Er, no, Master Oliver, you most certainly can't,' snapped Professor Cortex. He moved the poo-cam out of Ollie's reach. 'These are top secret spying devices, not for tricks in the playground. But,' he announced, 'I do have something to show you that does have relevance to the playground. Follow me and I'll show you an invention that is going to revolutionize learning around the globe.'

The professor led the Cooks down a maze of brilliant white corridors, past dozens of scientists hurrying about their duties. He stopped at a door marked 'Top Secret'.

'Wow!' whispered Ben to his sister. 'This invention must be really important to be in the top secret room in a top secret bunker in a top secret Spy School.'

The professor turned to the family, suddenly looking rather stern. 'What you are about to see is not to be repeated to anyone. Ever. Got it?'

The Cooks nodded. Sophie, Ollie and Ben were wide-eyed and speechless. The professor placed his identity card against a pad on the wall and the door swished open. The group assembled in what looked like an old-fashioned chemistry laboratory. There were bubbling potions of various colours, tubes linking glass vessels and steam rising from test tubes. Computers blinked and scientists hovered over experiments, some writing results and others adding ingredients. There was a whiteboard with complicated-looking formulae all over it.

Lara sniffed, her sensitive doggie nose taking in the unusual smells. *Candy floss?* she twitched. *And pancakes? It smells more like Willy Wonka's inventing room.*

'This, my friends, is the reason we've expanded to Spy School number two. My team and I,' he said, swooshing his arm around the room, 'have invented something rather spectacular. Something that is worth billions but, more importantly, something that will change the world.'

Crikey, thought Lara. *What is this major breakthrough, Prof?*

'Now where are they?' fussed Professor Cortex, rummaging through the pile of papers on the desk. 'They can't have gone far. I had them just a minute ago.' He reached into his pocket and pulled out yet another small electronic device. 'This should do the trick.' He pressed one of the buttons and looked at the screen. 'Ahhh,' he sighed. 'Silly me. They've been up there all the time.' He reached up and slid his spectacles from the top of his head down to his nose. 'I have a homing device fitted,' he smiled, peering over the top of his glasses. 'That way I can always find my specs. Smart or what? As I said, all the best inventions are basically very simple.'

Sophie jabbed her older brother in the ribs. 'Told you he was barmy,' she whispered.

'Now this is my latest and most awesome invention,' continued the professor proudly, holding up a test tube of purple liquid. He looked round at the collective wide eyes and beamed. 'This, my friends, is an intelligence formula. You may not be aware, GM451, but when you were a puppy you had an earlier version of this sprinkled on your cornflakes.  I've finally completed the experiments and the results are astonishing. Take a look at this,' he said, holding up a drawing of a monkey. 'This is a self-portrait by Annette, my cleverest chimp. What a talent.' Next he held up an A4 notebook. 'And this is her book of poetry,' smiled the professor.

The children were flabbergasted. 'And what's that cat doing?' asked Sophie, pointing to a cat holding a long stick.

'Oh, that's Connie,' explained the professor. 'An exceptional feline. Have you caught anything yet, Connie?' he shouted across the room.

The cat lifted her

fishing rod out of the indoor pond and shook her head. 'We're teaching Connie to catch her own supper,' said Professor Cortex. 'But it looks like the blighters aren't biting. The problem is that we've fed the fish on the brain formula as well, so they are getting too clever to catch. You've heard that fish live in schools? Well, ours really do. And they seem to have learnt how to avoid being caught. Most frustrating for Connie.'

The children's saucer eyes said it all. 'Really, Professor?' asked Ben. 'You've created intelligent goldfish?'

The scientist stroked his chin. 'It was a challenge I couldn't resist. Goldfish get such a bad press. A three-second memory indeed! Not *our* fish,' he chortled. 'They have better recall than me. We've started selling these intelligent fish in the pet superstore upstairs,' he said, jabbing his finger upwards. 'They're out there in fish tanks everywhere. Watching everything you do. Learning about the world.'

Ben could hardly contain his excitement. 'Does it work on humans? Can I try it?' he beamed.

'Humans?' repeated the professor, furrowing his brow. 'I've never considered using my brain formula on *humans*.' His brow creased until his eyebrows met in the middle. 'What a jolly interesting idea,' he reflected, twiddling his glasses. 'But no. Definitely not,' he barked.

'Why not?' asked Sophie. 'I mean, if it works on monkeys, then why not on people?'

'It's been developed for animals,' explained the professor. 'And it's perfectly safe for animals. It's impossible to predict what would happen if people took my formula.'

'I'd pass my exams without revising,' suggested Ben.

'And I'd win all the pub quizzes,' added Dad.

'And that'd be cheating,' snapped Professor Cortex, fixing his spectacles back on to his face. 'You should be ashamed of yourselves for even thinking it. But I bet you're not the only ones entertaining the idea. Imagine the advantages it would bring to the people who took it. And,' he added, his voice becoming serious, 'imagine what they'd be willing to pay for it.' The professor cast the family a knowing nod. 'Hence the need for secrecy,' he reminded them, tapping the side of his nose. 'Bob's your uncle.'

The family moved on while Ollie tried to work out what Uncle Bob had to do with it.

Professor Cortex completed his whirlwind tour of the Spy School, leaving the family shocked by some of the advances in technology. He was even in the middle of creating a robotic cleaner for the pet store, so no one would have to clean the animals' cages. The Cooks whizzed back to the exotic pets section and made their way out to the car, laden with gifts from the professor. Ben opened his goodie bag and smiled. 'Look, everyone, the professor's given me some night-vision goggles.'

Dad was really pleased with his remote control spectacles finder, and Sophie with her hat with built-in torch. Ollie was a little disappointed to be coming home without a pet zebra, but the professor had made it up to him with a football that contained a listening device. 'I'm going to kick it into next door's garden and spy on them,' he said excitedly.

Lara came away with a new collar, containing a screwdriver, torch and tin opener. She strapped herself into the people carrier and sat quietly. The visit had been exciting but she was disappointed that she might not be the world's cleverest animal any longer. *Monkeys writing poetry?* she thought. *And cats fishing for their own dinner?* Lara sighed. She was a family pet now and life was great. She knew the kids loved her no matter what. But she couldn't help feeling a little left out after seeing how the professor's work was charging ahead without her.

6. Ben's School Daze

Dame Payne waited impatiently while the children shuffled into the hall. It was their first assembly of the new school year. Ben stood awkwardly in his oversize blazer and shoes that were a size too big. He looked around at the scared faces and then at the unsmiling head teacher. It was her first day too. Ben wondered if she was nervous.

Dame Payne stood tall and gathered her black robes, flapping like a raven. She looked out at the sea of faces and wondered which child would become the superbrain.

'Blimey, check out her outfit. Looks like she thinks this is Hogwarts,' sniggered Toby Ward from Year Eight.

Dame Payne's hearing was as sharp as her temper. She pointed a warning finger at Toby. 'You, boy!' she shouted. 'The one laughing.'

Toby blushed. 'Who, me, Miss?' he mouthed, looking around innocently.

'Yes, you lad,' bellowed the new head. 'Out. Now. Pack your bags, clear your desk. You're finished.'

'But . . .' began Toby. 'I've not done nothing.'

'No. You haven't done *anything*,' corrected Dame Payne.

'Exactly,' agreed Toby Ward.

'Don't get clever with me, Sonny Jim,' warned the stern-faced head teacher. 'Did I ask you to answer back? No, I don't think I did. Goodbye, Mr Trouble.'

Silence fell as Toby Ward made his way out of the hall, the first innocent victim of the new regime.

Dame Payne waited until you could hear a pin drop. 'Welcome, everyone,' she said, smiling in all but her eyes. 'My name is Dame Payne and I am your new head teacher. I am here to develop some brilliant young brains.' She sneered. 'I know we will get along just fine so long as you abide by these few simple rules . . .'

'I can't believe how horrible she is,' complained Ben to his parents that evening. 'She's obsessed with growing everyone's brains. I've got masses of homework and it's only my first day,' he moaned. 'And Saturday school is just stupid.'

Lara let out a soft whistle. *Boy*, she thought, *that does sound tough*.

Dad nodded sympathetically. 'I know it may seem harsh,' he agreed, 'but I'm sure all the other schools are the same.'

'And no playtime,' added Ben. 'That's so unfair.'

'It does sound a little odd,' agreed Mum. 'But I think it's good that she wants to expand your brain. I'm sure she's doing it for a reason.'

'Oh, there's a reason all right,' retorted Ben. 'The teachers are trying to kill us, that's all. From exhaustion. She's expelled three people today. One for talking in assembly, one for asking for seconds at dinner and the other for complaining about having so much homework. It's awful, Dad. What am I going to do?'

I can help you with your homework, wagged Lara.

'There's not much you can do, mate,' said Dad. 'It's a good school. You were top of the Juniors so hang in there and you'll rise to the top again. I expect Dame Payne's just trying to maintain standards. Remember it was her first day too. Perhaps she'll ease off a bit when she's settled in. She's just trying to make an impression, that's all.'

'Well, she's done that all right!' muttered Ben, stamping out and slamming the door behind him. 'A horrible one!' they heard him shout as he trudged upstairs.

7. *Listening In*

Dad was right to say that Ben was one of the brightest in his class. He survived the first week under the new system but many didn't. Twenty per cent of his class members dropped off as they buckled under the strain. There was no talking back and very little fun. Those who complained were given extra homework.

There was no breaktime so Ben and his friends met in their secret spot in the cleaners' room to have a moan about things.

'It's so awful here,' complained Josh. 'I'm thinking of breaking the rules just so I can get thrown out. A transfer to another school sounds like a good option, even if it's miles away.'

'But what if it's worse?' suggested Ben.

'Impossible,' said Oscar. 'They won't have old "Payne in the neck". The woman's a nutter. She might get great results but there's no fun. You can't just rule by scaring everyone and working them into the ground. It's not right.'

'I'm struggling to keep up with the homework,' admitted Ben. 'I was up till midnight with science and only finished English at breakfast this morning.'

'Still straight A's, though, I bet,' said Oscar, smiling.

'Maybe, but I'll tell you what,' Ben added, forgetting what the professor had said about the need for secrecy, 'I wish I had the professor's brain formula. Then I'd be able to keep up, no problem.'

'A brain formula?' asked Josh, his eyes wide. 'That's just what I need. Come on, Ben, spill the beans. If I get kicked out of this school I'll be in serious trouble with my parents.'

Ben hesitated. It was supposed to be a secret but he knew Josh really was struggling with all the work. 'OK,' he said, 'but you all have to *promise* not to tell anyone about this.'

The boys agreed, so Ben went on to tell his mates about the secret laboratory under the pet supermarket. They skipped the entire geography lesson while he told them of the monkey poet and the cat that caught fish. Ben knew he should have kept the secret but was sure it would be safe with his best friends. Eventually the bell went and the three of them trudged off to Japanese.

Dame Payne sat at the bank of CCTV screens in her office. She considered that being a control freak was one of her better qualities. She liked to keep watch on everything and this was the best place. She'd got the whole school bugged. The head zoomed in on Miss Hutchins's maths class. All were sitting quietly as the teacher droned on about equations.

'Excellent,' she purred. 'Drill it into them, Miss Hutchins. Grow those brains.'

She spotted three lads in the cleaners' room on the first floor and glanced at her watch. 'Year Sevens,' she said, surprised. The time-table on the wall confirmed her suspicions. 'I smell trouble. They should be in geography,' she murmured. Dame Payne used the remote to zoom in and turn up the volume. She was disappointed to see Ben Cook skipping lessons, especially as his was one of the brains in the early running for selection. But then she heard Ben explain his story to Oscar and Josh. Her eyes lit up and she rubbed her chin thoughtfully. 'A brain formula. I don't believe it. Sounds like there may be a team of scientists ahead of us. That'll never do.' It didn't take long for a plan to start forming in her mind. Her eyes almost smiled as she broke away from the screens and tapped out a coded email to the other teachers. The head teacher's nose twitched in excitement as an emergency meeting was set for that night.

The teachers met in the executive meeting room at a posh hotel. 'Delighted you could all make it at such short notice,' Dame Payne began. 'I have some breaking news that I wanted to share urgently.' She put on an extra-serious face. 'This could change everything.' Then she pressed the button on her laptop and beamed a video clip on to the big screen. The members of the committee sat quietly, some nodding enthusiastically, as they watched the clip of Ben and his friends discussing the brain formula. 'So, ladies and gentlemen, I thought you should be aware of this major breakthrough,' she concluded. 'It seems as though there may be a scientific team ahead of us in this very important race. I propose we maintain our original plan, but that we investigate this "professor" as a possible plan B.'

'But is the boy reliable?' asked Mr Stern. 'It could just be a tall story.'

'Ben is in my form and I've already checked him out because he was showing signs of promise,' said Mr Wilde. 'He may even be the chosen one. He seems decent enough. And he's exceptionally bright.' He pressed a button to reveal the next slide, a huge picture of Ben lighting up the wall. 'Nice family,' continued

Mr Wilde as the Cooks were beamed on to
the big screen. 'Decent house. Live in a quiet
neighbourhood. Apparently he's got a really
clever dog. Rescued a drowning kid, so I hear.
Not sure if that's relevant or not.' Lara's picture
was next on to the screen, her bullet-holed ear
standing tall, the other drooping ridiculously.
'Strange-looking mutt, I must say. The
important thing is that this boy has no track
record as a liar.'

'OK,' said Mrs Grey. 'I suggest we get a
person on the inside of this laboratory to
check it out. If the story's true we can steal
their formula. And, in the meantime, we
accelerate our plan and identify the chosen
one as soon as possible.'

'Agreed,' nodded Dame Payne. 'It seems
we are in a race to create this super formula.
Can anyone name the second man on the

moon?' The head teacher raised herself to her full height as she surveyed the shaking heads. 'Exactly!' she bellowed. 'I doubt anyone will be interested in the team that comes second.'

'But getting someone on the inside of this place may be tricky. Who do we know who would stoop to such low levels? We're talking about fraud and theft here, ladies and gentlemen,' added Miss Hutchins from the back.

'Theft for a good and honourable purpose, though,' assured Dame Payne. 'We are like modern-day Robin Hoods. We steal from the rich and give to the poor . . . That is, the poor little blighters who need good exam results.' She smiled unpleasantly. 'We'll try to steal this formula and continue with our own experiments as well. Always nice to have a backup.'

Ben's science teacher raised his hand. 'Yes, Mr Wilde?' chirped the head.

'We need someone on the inside. Someone as dishonest as the day is long,' he growled. 'Someone who would sell their grandmother for a bag of sweets. Leave it with me. I have just the person in mind.'

8. The New Recruit

The professor's plans to build a robotic cleaner had been put on hold while he sorted out a glitch with the first one he'd created. The robot insisted on cleaning everything it saw, and no one could get any work done with a feather duster in their face every five minutes. 'It does the job brilliantly,' explained one of the team. 'It's just a little over-enthusiastic. I dropped my car keys yesterday and, quick as a flash, they were hoovered up!' Professor Cortex had no choice but to advertise for a part-time cleaner while he tweaked his invention. He was irritated that people were complaining about his robot and annoyed further when he found out that only one person had applied for the cleaning job.

Christopher Bent arrived in reception and

Professor Cortex watched him on the CCTV camera. The professor's nose scrunched up in disgust as the boy stuck a finger in his ear and started rummaging. Then he winced as the teenager examined the result and wiped his finger under the seat. 'Not ideal,' admitted Professor Cortex under his breath as he observed Bent's scruffy appearance and constant scratching. 'But then he's the only applicant, so I suppose beggars can't be choosers.'

The interview was rather painful. The professor was amazed by the teenager's lack of skills and ambition. He marvelled at the number of piercings, imagining that Bent would never make it through an airport metal detector without setting off the alarm. Even his tattoos were spelt wrongly. But his team desperately needed a cleaner so he'd have to give Bent a try until he could find someone better.

And so the school teachers' mole was in. Bent was well known to Mr Wilde, having caused him problems in the past with his disruptive and criminal behaviour. He was totally dishonest, had no friends and was an excellent thief. He had dropped out of school and, by all accounts, was a waster. 'Perfect for what we want,' was how Mr Wilde had described him.

Christopher Bent was recruited for the early and late shift, cleaning the pet superstore before opening and then coming back later. It gave him the perfect opportunity to snoop, find out any secrets and report back to the committee. Each evening he was to email a report to them, highlighting what he'd seen and heard. The lady with the sharp nose had been a bit vague but had said if he saw any interesting or unusual liquids then he was to steal them. It was made clear that he would be handsomely rewarded.

Bent wasn't really sure what he was supposed to be looking for. The lady had told him to keep his eyes peeled for any unusual behaviour but, to him, everything about this pet shop was weird. He noticed early on that a lot of staff came through the door in the morning, but not many worked in the shop. It was as if they were disappearing somewhere.

On his second day, as Bent swept up at the far end of the shop, he noticed it was the exotic animals' area that most of the staff headed to. He put his brush down and sneaked into one of the nearby dog kennels to watch. Before long a smartly dressed lady marched down the shop, right past his kennel and into the exotic animals' corner. She stroked a parrot's beak and Bent rubbed his eyes in disbelief as the floor started to sink and the lady disappeared. 'Wow!' he gasped. 'Watch out for anything unusual. It doesn't come any weirder than that. I must get to know Polly Parrot . . .'

Christopher Bent was deliberately late for his evening shift. He apologized to his supervisor. 'I'll work a bit longer tonight to make up,' he volunteered. His boss was happy with this solution and so his plan was in action.

Bent swept the floor and hovered, keeping one eye on the staff as they left the building. By eight o'clock he reckoned there was hardly anyone left. 'Here goes,' he whispered to himself, his heart beating fast. He'd watched at least twenty people disappear underground today and could hardly wait to try it himself. He took Professor Cortex's ID card from his pocket and smiled to himself. It had been fairly easy to pick the professor's pocket – he'd pretended to bump into him as he left work that night. 'The silly old fool won't realize until tomorrow,' he grinned, pleased that his days of petty crime were about to pay off after all.

Bent continued sweeping as he made his way into the exotic animals' corner, head down but eyes darting all around. There didn't appear to be anyone watching so he quickly tapped the parrot's beak. His ears popped as the platform descended into the secret underground bunker.

The lift stopped and Bent stepped off, still sweeping. If he got caught he intended to say that he had no idea how he'd got there – one minute he was cleaning the parrot's cage and the next second he was here. Thankfully, there was no one around so he carried his broom down the long white corridor, padding silently, the hairs on the back of his neck standing on end. 'Which door do I choose?' he thought. Suddenly he heard footsteps and swung into a nearby room. A man and a woman wearing white coats were in the middle of some sort of experiment. They looked up but carried on working.

'Er, just making sure everything is spick and span,' Bent explained, sweeping busily. *This must be some sort of laboratory*, he thought to himself as he looked around.

The footsteps passed and he went back to the corridor, hurrying down the passageway. He stopped in front of the final door, his hands shaking with excitement. 'Top Secret' said the notice. 'This must be it,' he thought. He leant his broom against the wall and took the professor's ID card out of his pocket. As soon as he pressed the card against the panel, the door slid open. Bent looked right and left before scurrying through with his broom. He breathed a sigh of relief as he entered the room.

Inside there were test tubes filled with all sorts of coloured potions, and Bunsen burners glowed underneath glass jars containing bubbling liquids. In the background a whole bank of computers flickered. Bent was surprised to see half a dozen monkeys tucked up in a bed with an A4 pad covered in drawings and poetry. He noticed a small box on the table with a big 'Do not touch' label stuck to it. He crept over to look. 'Poo-cam?' he read. 'The lady said to steal whatever I could so I'll pocket one of those.'

His eyes followed a series of pipes and levers before coming to rest on a test tube of purple liquid. He tiptoed over to the liquid and sniffed. It had a sweet aroma. He looked at the label stuck to the tube. 'Brain formula' it said in bold letters. Bent let out a gasp. 'Oh, boy,' he said. 'Brain formula! This must be what the lady's after.' He took a cork and stuffed it into the top of the test tube. Then

he pocketed it and backed out of the top-secret laboratory, picking up his broom once more. The two scientists he'd seen earlier came round the corner.

'There you are,' said the man.

'We've come to check you are allowed down here,' said the woman. 'This is a restricted area, you know.'

'Oh, soz,' gulped Christopher Bent. 'I was just sweeping up, that's all. Professor Cortex asked me to clean in here.' He hoped if he mentioned the professor's name they would leave him alone.

'Can I see your ID?' said the male scientist cautiously.

'Haven't got any ID,' replied the teenager, thinking as quickly as his slow mind could. 'I'm new, you see.'

'So how did you get down here without ID?' asked the woman suspiciously.

Bent's pea-sized brain couldn't cope with a question like that, so before long he was being ushered into a room and told to wait while someone called security. He sighed as he heard the door lock. He knew his story wouldn't add up. He didn't want to be caught with the evidence, so he took the test tube from his pocket and uncorked it. He sniffed once more. 'Smells OK,' he thought, his nose twitching. 'And I could certainly do with some brain power right now.'

He put the sweet liquid to his lips and downed it, spluttering a bit as the top-secret formula slid down his throat. His eyes rolled and his head shook a couple of times. He blinked and finished with an enormous belch – a purple one! 'Wow, that's good stuff,' he gasped. He rinsed the test tube and sat down just as the security guard entered.

Christopher Bent was searched and found to be in possession of a stolen poo-cam. He was sacked that night and banned from the building. Professor Cortex was worried Bent would let out the secret of what was hidden below the pet shop. But then he remembered that the teenager had trouble remembering his own name. He doubted anyone would believe him anyway.

'Get your hands off me,' Bent shouted as the security team ushered him into the car park. 'I ain't stolen anything,' he lied. 'I'm not stupid, you know.' That was also a lie. At that moment he was incredibly stupid. Christopher Bent's new brain power wouldn't kick in until the following morning. And when it did, there would be trouble ahead.

9. Clever Clogs

Christopher Bent slept most of the next day and didn't wake until late afternoon. He lay still for a few minutes, cursing the fact that he'd lost his job and wondering how he'd explain it to the teachers. Would he still get paid? He stumbled out of bed and looked in the mirror. 'Same ugly mug,' he thought. But he felt different. Sort of alive. He made a cup of tea and helped himself to a bowl of Frosties. He took his bowl into the lounge and flicked on the TV. *Countdown* was his favourite show, even though he was only good at making three-letter words. He'd once got a four-letter one but it was a swear word so it didn't count.

He stared at the row of vowels and consonants that Carol had arranged on the shelf. 'Intestine,' he muttered to himself. 'Dead easy.' He shovelled a big spoonful of Frosties into his mouth and crunched noisily.

The time was up and the contestants had both scored five. Even the lady with the dictionary hadn't got a nine-letter word. 'Intestine, you daft woman!' he shouted at the screen. 'Are you thick or what?' He frowned. 'Hang on,' he said to himself. 'How did I know that? I'm rubbish at this game.' Bent shook his head and continued to crunch on his cereal.

The contestants moved on to the numbers game. He hated it when a seventy-five came up. 'Rock hard,' he thought as Carol pressed the button and the number 616 appeared. He looked at the numbers and the spoon fell from his hand. '616,' he gasped aloud. He worked it through under his breath, all the pieces falling into place. 'Multiply the six and the nine, add the two. Then add the eight and three together. Then multiply eleven by fifty-six. 616. A doddle!' The teenager furrowed his brow. He'd always struggled with his two times table and now here he was, beating Carol at her own game. His Frosties went soggy as he sat glued to the TV, scoring maximum points for the rest of the game.

That evening Bent filed his email report. He was so proud of the way he could string sentences together. He had a big grin as he read the last sentence again. 'Big news to report so I need an urgent meeting with the committee.' He clicked 'Send'. 'Big news indeed,' he chuckled. 'I'm about to double-cross a bunch of teachers.'

Christopher Bent appeared before the school teachers the very next day. He sat, head bowed. 'Got sacked,' he said, deliberately avoiding eye contact.

'Unfortunate,' sneered Dame Payne, who wasn't really surprised. She gave him a piercing look. 'However, in your short time there did you see anything, you know, unusual?' she asked uncomfortably. 'Any strange liquids, for example?'

'Oh, yes. Lots of weird stuff going on there, lady,' replied Bent, making eye contact for the first time. 'There's this mad professor in charge. He's the big cheese down there. I think he's an inventor.' Bent slid a grainy photo of the professor across the table. 'I took this on my mobile,' he explained.

'Good work, Mr Bent,' purred the head teacher.

'Oh, but I did much better than that,' grinned the teenager, coming alive at last. He pulled a test tube from his pocket. 'I managed to steal this from a downstairs laboratory,' he boasted. 'As you can see –' he pointed to the label – 'it's the professor's secret brain formula. I'm guessing this is the kind of thing you were after?' He held the test tube out to the audience and they all leant in towards it. 'Something like this could change the world,' he said slowly and deliberately. 'But it'll cost ya.' He rested the test tube on his knee. 'Big time.'

Bent felt an icy atmosphere fall on the room. He looked at Dame Payne's forced smile and Mr Wilde's wonky grin. All eyes were fixed on the test tube. He moved the purple liquid from side to side and all eyes followed, like spectators at Wimbledon. He'd worked out it was the brain formula they were after so he'd created a fake one. He'd mixed honey, washing-up liquid and hair gel to form something really yucky. Well, he assumed it was yucky. The old Bent would have tasted it but the new one was far too clever. And they weren't to know it wasn't the real thing – that in fact he'd swallowed the true formula. They had no idea that he was now superintelligent – able to outsmart them – which was exactly what he was doing now.

Narrowing her eyes at him, Dame Payne made a call on her mobile. The room was deadly silent for the next ten minutes until

there was a knock on the door. A man in a suit entered, carrying a briefcase. 'Your extra money as requested, Dame Payne,' he explained, placing the bag on the table. He left the room and all eyes turned back to Bent.

The teenager smiled with satisfaction as the head woman handed over the briefcase of cash. 'Don't snatch, lady,' he warned as Dame Payne wrestled the test tube from his hands. But all she could do was stare at the formula as Christopher Bent was escorted off the premises by the two biggest teachers.

'Like taking candy off a baby,' he muttered on the way out.

10. Game On

Ben couldn't understand why all the school water fountains tasted funny. Some of them even blew bubbles instead of water. As a result, none of the children drank the foul-tasting stuff, choosing to buy the bottled variety from the school shop.

Dame Payne couldn't understand it either. She'd tipped the liquid into the school water supply. The aim was to share the brain formula all around the school and she was expecting a massive uplift in school performance as a result. She monitored the results closely and all she got were a few upset tummies, an increase in bottled water sales and some water fountains that blew bubbles. She'd even tasted the water herself and could understand why the kids were avoiding it. 'Ugh,' she grimaced,

wiping the taste from her lips and the bubbles from her chin. 'Tastes like honey and . . . and,' she said, rolling her tongue around her mouth, '. . . washing-up liquid?' She was impressed that the professor had come up with a brain formula but not so impressed that he couldn't make it taste nice. 'Still,' she thought, reflecting back to her childhood, 'all medicine tastes horrid. If it tastes this bad then it must be doing me some good.'

As head of science, she'd instructed Mr Wilde to undertake some scientific experiments on the liquid. 'We need to know the active ingredient. And quickly,' she'd ordered.

The school regime didn't improve. Ben and his classmates were thoroughly miserable, working long hours in and out of school. Lara was worried about him. They hardly ever had time to play football or go fishing and Ben had become sullen and quiet. Lara thought the rules were unusually harsh and, as far as she could tell, homework grades didn't seem to be better than the other schools. If anything, many of the children were suffering from exhaustion and results would go the wrong way.

'We have to relax and have fun sometimes,' Ben complained to his parents. 'We'd work so much harder if we were allowed a break.'

Unfortunately for Ben, his results had stayed strong, meaning he was now head and shoulders above the rest. It seemed as though he was destined to be the chosen one.

Dame Payne logged off her laptop. It was Saturday night and she'd spent fourteen hours studying children's performance. There appeared to be one child who was brilliant across the board and she was happy that Benjamin Cook would be nominated as the superbrain. He was a fine specimen – she was sure the other teachers would agree.

The head teacher flicked on the kettle and checked her text messages while it boiled. She thumbed through a message from Mr Wilde.

Experiments dun. Active ingredients hunny, wash-up liqid + hair gel. Weird

'Weird indeed,' she agreed, stirring her coffee. Dame Payne was deep in thought as she sank into her favourite armchair and switched on the TV. She hardly heard the familiar theme tune to *Who Wants to Be a Millionaire?* She was still thinking of honey and hair gel so she missed the host's sprightly introduction and fifteen new contestants waving enthusiastically. Her attention became focused when she heard the name 'Christopher Bent'.

'That's the fastest finger ever,' beamed the host as he pumped Bent's hand up and down. 'Come and take your place in the hot seat.'

Dame Payne perched on the edge of her chair as Bent flew through to £32,000 without using a single lifeline. He asked the audience on £64,000. The audience got it wrong but Professor Cortex's temporary cleaner got it right. There was a huge round of applause as he progressed on to £125,000. He hesitated at a quarter of a million. 'I'm not so good on the history of art,' he'd said bashfully. But 50:50 had narrowed it down and he'd plumped for the right answer. Half a million was tricky but he flew through it.

'You've still got Phone a Friend,' reminded the host.

'To be honest,' Bent smiled, 'I don't actually have any friends.' The audience laughed. *He's so modest*, they thought. *And so intelligent. I bet he has loads of lovely mates.*

Dame Payne's lips pursed tighter as Bent reached the million-pound question. Bent

knew the answer to the biggest question of his life before the answers had been revealed, but he wanted this to be good viewing so he spent an age weighing up the options. The host was sweating; the audience was willing him on. Hardly anyone ever won the big prize. Bent knew it was B but skirted round the answers, nearly plumping for A and then D. 'I think I'll have a guess at B,' he said eventually.

The host winced. 'Final answer?' he asked. If you're wrong you will lose your half million. Remember, you don't have to play.'

Bent thought of the millions of people watching around the country and milked the TV exposure. 'It's only a game,' he beamed. 'B . . . final answer.'

Answer B went orange. There was no changing now. The audience held their breath and Bent tried to look nervous, knowing only too well that he was now a millionaire.

The host put on a downbeat voice. 'So you, Christopher Bent, unemployed from Derby, came here with nothing. You worked your way to the million-pound question and answered B . . . "King Hussein of Jordan".'

Yes, get on with it, man, thought Bent. *Just give me my dosh.*

'You have just . . .' continued the host, teasing the audience. 'Just . . .' he said, looking directly at camera one, 'just WON one million pounds!'

The studio audience erupted, and confetti and balloons fell from the studio ceiling. The producer was delighted to have the opportunity of finally pulling the lever.

Dame Payne sat stony-faced as she watched five minutes of backslapping and handshaking, before the host and Christopher Bent waved goodnight to the nation.

The TV clicked off and the room fell eerily silent. Dame Payne perched like a bird of prey, fixing the blank TV with a determined stare. It was obvious she'd been tricked. 'Bent's taken the formula and sold us a dummy,' she thought aloud. 'I suppose that explains the hair gel. But he's transformed himself from dunce to genius, so at least he's proved the professor's formula works.' She smiled to herself. Dame Payne was beyond anger. She felt calm. Her next step was obvious.

11. A Pain in the Backside

Even though it was Saturday night, Professor Cortex was working in the lab, tweaking his automatic cleaning device. He'd asked the chimps to get their pyjamas on and get themselves tucked up in bed. 'If you're good,' he promised, 'I'll let you watch *Millionaire*.' The professor had never seen the chimps get ready for bed so quickly. Since they'd been taking their brain formula they couldn't get enough of game shows. They jumped up and down on their beds when the theme tune came on and the professor raised a 'get back into bed or the TV goes off' eyebrow. All was peaceful for five minutes as he busied himself with an experiment. But his attention was drawn by someone getting the fastest finger ever. His jaw dropped as he watched

Christopher Bent take the hot seat. 'It's him,' he said, pointing at the screen. 'That awful man who we sacked last week. Well, he doesn't stand a chance because he's the most stupid person I've ever met.'

The professor's mouth continued to widen in disbelief as he watched Christopher Bent scoop the million-pound prize. And he didn't need any brain formula to work out that Bent had stolen his secret.

Professor Cortex was the last out of the pet shop. He had no idea he was being watched as he locked up and made his way across the car park to his van.

The gunman had made himself comfortable on the roof of the furniture warehouse across the road. He saw the professor and shook himself awake. This was the moment he'd been waiting for. He fixed a dart to his rifle, put his eye to the sight and focused on the old man. He aimed the cross at his chest before finally settling on his leg. The man's finger eased on to the trigger. He knew he'd only get one shot.

The professor never dawdled. Life was one

long emergency and his legs moved quickly as he scurried across the car park.

The hit man cursed. 'Slow down, old boy,' he whispered. 'I want to get a clean shot.'

The professor fumbled for his keys, finding them and then dropping them. 'Oh bother. What a butterfingers.' He put his briefcase down and bent to feel underneath his car. This was the moment. The hit man aimed at the professor's upturned bottom and squeezed the trigger.

A poison dart sailed through the air and landed right on target.

Professor Cortex felt a bee sting. 'Ouch, my bum,' he exclaimed, before hitting the tarmac with a thud.

12. Keeping the Secret

Christopher Bent sat in his new luxury apartment, wallowing in his wealth. He was wearing the latest designer gear and had surrounded himself with electronic gadgets, many still in their boxes. His superintelligence had brought him supreme wealth, but it couldn't buy him friends to share it with.

He flicked on the huge surround-sound TV. It was *Countdown* time again. He loved the programme, now that he could outsmart the presenters. Bent lay full length on his leather couch and tapped along with the theme tune. The first round was tricky. Bent was disappointed to get only a three-letter word when the contestants got six. Round two was worse. He got 'hat' when the contestants got 'although'. 'What's going on?'

he said aloud. 'Come on, Chrissy, where's your genius today?'

The numbers round was a nightmare. He was miles away from the answer. 'No, no, no, you stupid telly,' he bellowed, jumping off the couch and slamming his foot through the screen. The wide-screen TV fizzed as glass shattered everywhere and Bent fell to the floor clutching his foot. 'My cleverness is fading,' he sobbed. 'I can't go back to being thick. I'll have to find that mad professor and get more brain formula.'

Professor Cortex woke up in a bed. Crisp white sheets covered him and light was streaming through the window. He felt groggy. He wasn't wearing his glasses so the room was blurred, but he could see someone standing by the bed. 'Hello,' croaked the professor. 'I'm sorry to bother you, but where am I?'

'Good afternoon, Professor,' a female voice replied. 'You have been transferred from one special agency to another. We would like to employ you to produce your brain formula especially for us. Then we will sell the rights to your product around the world. We want

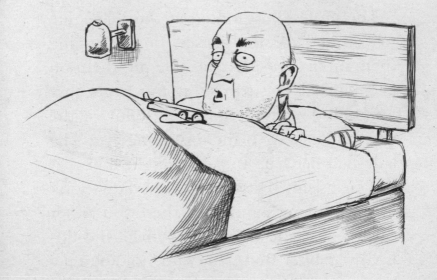

the secret of what happened to Christopher Bent.'

The professor's head pounded, the poison from the dart still swimming round his bloodstream. 'Brain formula?' he murmured, trying to sound surprised. He watched the blurred figure nodding. 'Who are you?' he asked. 'Where am I? And who may I ask is Christopher Bent?'

'The "who" and "where" doesn't matter right now, Professor Cortex,' soothed the voice. 'You are perfectly safe and will be treated like a king. You have a secret. As soon as you've shared that secret with us you are free to go.'

The professor squinted at the shape. He felt around for his glasses, finally finding them on his bedside table. He put them on and blinked in surprise at the large nose pointing directly at him. He followed the nose all the way to the unsmiling eyes. The lady had her hair in such a tight bun that her face seemed stretched. She didn't look like an enemy agent but then you never could tell in the world of spying. 'And this is Christopher Bent,' she said, holding up a tabloid newspaper. 'Former thickie scoops jackpot,' screamed the headline, showing the professor's cleaner plastered across the front page.

'Oh, deary me,' sighed the professor, his head throbbing. 'He obviously stole my formula.'

The lady's lips turned up at the corners but her cold eyes bored into the professor. She nodded. 'And now my colleagues and I must have the secret. For the good of the world, you understand. Ours is a just cause, Professor.'

Professor Cortex nodded. He was too tired to put up a fight. Surely somebody would notice he was missing and alert GM451? He closed his eyes and drifted back to sleep. He just hoped that GM451 would be able to rescue him before they forced him to reveal his life's work.

13. Saving Ben

The professor was set up in a new laboratory. He had everything he wanted, except his freedom. He even had a great view because the teachers had set up his new lab on the top floor of a luxury hotel, away from prying eyes. The doors were bolted and there was no way he could escape from a room that was twenty-three floors up. To make absolutely sure, Dame Payne had provided a minder called Len whose head looked like a potato. He was so big he almost filled the doorway.

The professor was visited by Dame Payne and Mr Wilde. 'I thought I ought to check you've settled in,' said the head teacher, struggling to be friendly. 'And my head of science, Mr Wilde, will act as your assistant during your stay with us.'

'Why exactly am I here?' inquired the professor, glancing at the man-mountain blocking his escape route. 'I don't want to work for another secret agency – I need to go back to the Spy School and finish *my* work.' He looked around the hotel room. 'The animals will miss me,' he pleaded. 'I'm part of a team and they'll worry when I'm not there.'

Dame Payne cut him off. 'My committee will give you one week, Professor. All you have to do is re-create your brain formula. And then you can go free.'

'And if I won't?' asked the professor. 'Or can't?'

Len stepped forward and gave his best sneer. The professor winced as the thug cracked his knuckles.

'If you *won't*, it becomes Len's business,' said Dame Payne, dropping her attempt at friendliness. 'If you *can't*, then my team moves to plan B.'

'Which is?'

'Let's just say we're close to completing a brain formula of our own. All we need is the brain of a child, and you'll be pleased to

know that we've selected the most intelligent pupil in our school. A boy called Benjamin Cook.'

The professor's face went purple with rage. 'You've what?' he spluttered. He couldn't let on that he knew Ben, but the very thought of taking someone's brain made him angry enough.

'Selected Benjamin Cook's brain,' repeated Dame Payne icily. 'But you can save the boy, Professor. In fact, you're the only one who can. If you provide us with your formula we will have no need for the child's brain.'

The professor mopped his brow. His colour had drained from purple to white. He was shaking but managed a weak smile. 'We'd best get busy then, Mr Wilde,' he said, booting up his laptop. 'If I want to save Ben's life. May I ask what you want the formula for? Other than the fact it's worth millions?'

'I think you may have answered your own question, Professor,' asserted Dame Payne. 'All you need to know is that you have one week to re-create your brilliant formula.'

No, thought the professor. *Someone will alert GM451 and all I need to do is stall as long as possible, until she comes to my rescue.* He wasn't quite sure how she'd rescue him, but he was confident that as soon as she knew he was missing she would.

Christopher Bent was focused on getting his hands on more brain formula. He lay full length on his sofa and put the sleek mobile to his ear. It rang three times before the answerphone kicked in. Bent stayed cool. 'It's me,' he said calmly. 'It's clear we're both after the same thing. The intelligence formula is worth millions. How about we help each other out and share the proceeds 50:50? Ring me, urgently.'

14. Bent Double With Payne

Later that night Dame Payne sat silently at the kitchen table, her microwave whirring in the background. She was shaking with excitement as she replayed Christopher Bent's message one more time. She ran through her thoughts out loud. 'It's all there for the taking, and Bent is bad enough to do the dirty work. We will kidnap the mad professor again, so he can produce the formula just for me.' Her evil face broke into a genuine smile for the first time in years. 'And I don't see why I have to share it with anyone.'

The microwave pinged and Dame Payne removed her 'lasagne for one'. She reached for her mobile and tapped a message for Christopher Bent.

Prof held top floor palace hotel. Meet me
there 4pm 2moro. Profits split 50:50

Then one more message, this time for Len,
asking him to run an errand at four o'clock
the next day. *That's the minder out of the way*,
she thought as she took a spoon and greedily
attacked her pasta.

Lara took an early morning phone call from
the Secret Service. Ben could tell it was
serious. 'What's up, girl?' he asked. His pet
secured a pencil in her mouth and scribbled
some letters on a pad.

'The professor's missing!' yelled Ben. 'What
do you mean, "missing"? Where can he be?'

Where indeed? pondered Lara. She knew
the old man lived for his work. He only left
the office to sleep and eat, even choosing to
stay overnight on a camp bed in the lab on
some occasions. *I guess there could be a simple
explanation*, she thought. *I mean, he could be
on a holiday or visiting friends.* Deep down she
knew this was unlikely. The professor never
had holidays and didn't have any friends,
except his animals.

'We need to find him,' said Ben as he and Lara sat at the kitchen table. Lara was helping the boy with his science homework, which seemed terribly difficult. She had watched poor Ben become more and more stressed with school as the work piled up. And now they needed to find the professor too. *But where do we start looking?* she wondered.

Lara had an idea. She tugged at Ben's jeans and beckoned him into the lounge where her Harry Potter book was. She sat down before reaching for her reading glasses and putting them on.

Ben frowned. 'Well, I hardly think it's time to read books, Lara. I mean, the prof might

be in big trouble. He needs us to help, not chill out.'

The glasses, thought Lara, peering over the rim. *The prof's glasses have a homing device. Remember Spy School? We just need to find the gadget that tracks the specs. Find the specs and we find the mad scientist. Do you understand me? What do you say?*

Ben looked blank. Lara took off her specs and waved them in the air. *The glasses, lad. The prof's glasses, not mine.* She jumped off the chair and went over to a picture of herself and the professor. She pointed her paw at the man and then waved the glasses again. *Get it? Homing glasses*, she urged.

Ben twigged. 'Gotcha, Lara,' he yelled. 'The professor has a homing device fitted to his specs.'

And the prof gave Dad one when we visited the Spy School, remember?

'Dad's homing device,' yelled Ben, putting his hand up like at school. He pounded upstairs to Mum and Dad's bedroom and rummaged for the goodie bag that Dad had brought back from the Spy School. 'This should tell us,' he sang, waving the iPod-looking gadget in the air. Ben touched the small screen and the tracker sprang into life. Soon he and Lara were working their way through the menu, clicking on the icon for 'professor's spectacles'.

The next day, Ben, Sophie, Ollie and Lara turned up at the Palace Hotel. They gazed at the huge glass building stretching into the sky and then down at the tracking device. 'His glasses are in there somewhere,' said Ben. 'So logic says the professor must be in there too.'

'Let's go and ask, then,' suggested Sophie, walking towards the door. The children were stopped by a doorman with a peaked cap. 'Definitely no pets and preferably no children,' he told them. 'Unless, of course, you're blind or royalty,' he said snootily.

'We've met the Queen,' offered Ollie.

'And I've met the Emperor of China,' smirked the doorman. 'Now hop it.'

'We're hoping to meet someone who's staying here,' explained Ben.

The doorman really wasn't keen on children. He looked at Lara and curled his lip. 'Shall I let you into a secret?' he said. 'I hate dogs.'

And I hate people who hate dogs, snapped Lara. *I'm tempted to take you out with a karate kick, but I guess that would only draw attention to us. So I'll stay calm and we'll go to plan B. See you later, doggie-hater.*

Lara led the children into the hotel car park. *OK, guys. I have a cunning plan. It's not perfect but I can't think of any other way in, and the prof needs rescuing sooner rather than later.* Lara undid Ben's backpack and took out her colourful tartan coat. She sighed heavily. *OK, guys,* she thought, *strap me in.*

Ben fitted the coat over his pet and admired his handiwork. 'There you go, girl,' he said, grinning. Lara sighed. 'Don't droop your ears like that. You look fine,' Ben fibbed.

Lara raised an eyebrow at him. *Like I believe that! But on with the job – stand back,* she woofed, forming a clear space around her. *This may work, but it also has the potential to go horribly wrong.* Lara looked up at the twenty-three gleaming floors above. She spied an open window on the ninth floor and hoped she would have enough rope.

The children's faces were anxious as they watched her prepare.

'Are you sure you can do this?' asked Sophie, biting her bottom lip. 'That window is a long way up.'

Lara shrugged. *I guess we'll never know till we try*, she considered. *Here goes. It's going to be a giant leap for dog-kind.* Lara took a deep breath and took aim. She pressed the button and the grappling hook shot out, high into the air. The children held their breath as the hook soared through the open window. They heard a distant clank and Lara tugged at the rope, making sure it was secure. *OK*, she thought, fixing her helmet in place, *now this is the tricky bit. Wish me luck.* Lara took an even deeper breath and pressed the second button. Her head jerked and her body followed as the mechanism pulled her upwards at an alarming rate.

The children watched as Lara took off, her howling getting fainter as she rose high above them. They held their breath as she banged against the open window then reached over to it with one paw. Sophie squealed as Lara's other paw scraped at the

glass, her back legs kicking, trying to swing in through the half-open window.

'Go on, Lara,' urged Ben.

The family pet pulled with all her might. She swung on the rope until finally she was able to scramble through the window. The children breathed a collective sigh of relief as they watched her back legs disappear.

Dame Payne and Christopher Bent waited for Len to disappear on his shopping errand. Mr Wilde had spent a lifetime with his head in textbooks rather than at the gym. As a result, Bent easily overpowered him and very quickly secured him to a chair. His shouting was a problem so Bent stuffed a pair of socks into his mouth.

Dame Payne turned her attention to Professor Cortex. 'There's been a change of plan,' she announced.

Bent sneered. 'Yeah,' he nodded, 'we don't want to share the profits for your formula with anyone else. We've decided you can make it for us. In an exclusive deal.'

'And why would I do that?' demanded the professor.

Dame Payne smiled icily. 'Because it's no different from what you're doing now – the alternative still involves taking the brain of an innocent child. And you don't want that to happen now, do you? So we're leaving for somewhere a bit more secret. You get to weave your magic and save Ben Cook . . . and we become billionaires!'

The professor had no time to think it through. He clutched his laptop tightly as he followed Dame Payne and Christopher Bent into the lift.

15. Room Service

Lara landed in a hotel bedroom with a thump. *Phew*, she gasped. *That was close.* She heard the toilet flush and a man wandered out of the bathroom. He was an elderly gentleman with a giant mop of black hair. *Clearly a wig*, thought Lara. *And I don't need secret agent training to work that out!*

He did a double take when he saw Lara. 'Er, a dog,' he said aloud. 'What's a dog doing in my room?' He blinked hard. 'And why has it got a helmet on?' he added as an afterthought.

Lara wagged her tail as she let herself out into the corridor, following her highly trained nose. She was no longer a family pet – she was a Spy Dog again. Her heart was racing, her mind keeping pace with it. She wriggled out of her ridiculous coat and lost the helmet. *Lift or stairs?* she thought. *Humans are lazy so nearly always travel by lift*, she reckoned. *Therefore I've got a better chance of secret snooping if I take the stairs.* She nosed into the stairwell, which was empty, and trotted up a few flights, nose to the ground. *Where on earth do I start looking? He could be anywhere.* She sniffed again, hoping to pick up the professor's scent. There was something unusual coming from upstairs. *Up we go.*

Lara bounded up the stairs, the smell getting stronger. She stood on the twenty-third floor, panting heavily. *Perhaps the lift would be better next time. This is it*, she thought as she nosed the door open and crept through. Lara did a double take at the scene. She wasn't in a hotel room; she was in what looked like a laboratory. And a man with angry eyes was tied to a chair. *It's not the prof, but maybe he can help*, Lara hoped.

The man's face was bright red and he was shouting in a muffled voice. It took Lara a while to realize he had socks stuffed in his mouth. She bounded over to the man and pulled them out with her teeth. The man didn't look very impressed as his face was covered with Lara's doggie slobber.

Oops, sorry about the tuna sandwich I had for lunch, yapped Lara. *Just be grateful you can speak again, mister. Hey, don't I know you from somewhere?*

'Help!' bellowed Mr Wilde. 'Someone help me.'

Well, I'll help you if you stop bellowing like that, thought Lara. *Where's the professor?*

The man shouted again, obviously unaware that Lara was a superdog. 'If only you could untie me, mutt,' he gasped. 'There's an evil dame, a stupid man and a mad professor who've just left. They've struck a deal. They have a secret that they're going to sell for millions – perhaps billions! I've been double-crossed. They're all in it together and I have to stop them!'

It sounded like Lara was in the right place, just moments too late. Then she stopped in her tracks. *Pardon, sir?* she thought. *Did you say they are in it together? That would make the professor a baddie. I really don't think so.*

The man yelled for help again before telling himself off. 'I should have seen it coming,' he groaned. 'I can't believe they've left me out. I bet that mad professor turns out to be as greedy as the others.'

Lara was wide-eyed. *Surely not,* she thought. *There must be some mistake. The professor wouldn't sell out. He's a good guy.*

Lara looked at the prisoner and considered her options. It would take ages to untie him by which time the professor would be long gone. If she was to rescue the professor and stop the criminal gang she had to act now. *Sorry, sir,* she woofed, doing her best sad eyes. *I've got a mystery to solve. But I'll come back for you later, honest.* With that, Lara raced out of the door and pressed the 'Lift down' button.

Come on, come on, she muttered to herself as she watched the dial coming up, then stopping, then coming up a bit more. Eventually the lift pinged and the doors swished open.

'Blast! I thought this lift was going down –' The elderly man with the wig was shocked into silence when Lara got into the lift. He looked even more surprised when she pressed the 'G' button and accompanied him to the ground floor. 'I really must remember to speak to Doctor Johnson about my medication,' he murmured to himself.

Come on, come on, thought Lara, tapping her paw impatiently as the lift descended. *I need to make up time. Not lose it*. The doors opened and Lara sprinted, greyhound-style, into the hotel lobby. She raced past reception, knocked over a waiter and dodged a group of American tourists who were milling about. The man with the uniform was guarding the door. He saw Lara coming.

'You again,' he mouthed. Lara read his lips. 'I hate dogs.'

Yes, me again, thought Lara. *What are you*

going to do about it? She stopped in her tracks and looked all around. There seemed to be only one way out and the dog-hater was guarding it.

'A dog on the loose!' yelled a woman. All eyes turned to Lara.

'Get that dog out of here!' screamed the manager.

Calm down, everyone. There's no need to panic, Lara assured them. *And I'm not dangerous. Unless you're a baddie, of course.* She spied Dame Payne and Christopher Bent hurrying out of the main entrance, taking advantage of the confusion to make their escape. The professor scurried after them. *Oh, my goodness,* she gasped. *Surely the man wasn't right. But why is the professor escaping with those baddies?* The security guard closed the door. *No time to think, just take action, Lara,* she told herself. *Remember your training.*

The guard seemed determined to be a bit of a hero. Everyone else had run away, but he was striding towards her. 'Come here, mutt,' he soothed.

I don't think so, thought Lara, her eyes darting everywhere, trying to spot an escape route. The doorman was closing in. She bolted into the hotel restaurant, following the man with the black wig. The doorman was now sprinting after her. She couldn't see a way out and was trapped. *Not a good move.* Lara backed into a corner as the guard approached. She issued a low warning growl. He picked up a chair and kept coming. Little did Lara know but this was the most exciting thing that had happened in his fifteen years as doorman of the hotel.

'Come on, poochie,' he coaxed, taking some sausages from a customer's plate and holding them out to Lara. 'Come and get your din dins.'

Oh, for heaven's sake, thought Lara. *The baddies are getting away with the country's top scientist and you want me to sit here eating sausages. The world is at stake, man. Get out of my way.* Lara hated to show off but there was no choice. She stood on her hind legs and took a step forward. She did a kick and a punch in the air. *I'm a black belt, matey*, she warned, bending her knees, ready to attack. *Don't mess with me.* The man looked surprised but continued towards her. Lara had to take a chance. *What can I throw?* she thought. *How can I create a diversion?*

She looked round at the customers, who'd all stopped eating and seemed very worried indeed. The man with the wig was seated at the next table. Lara approached him and stood up. *Excuse me*, she thought. *I need a diversion and you might have the answer.* The man looked terrified. Lara whipped off his wig and juggled with the hairy mop as if it were alive. *Yikes*, she yelped. *It looks like a hamster.*

The customers screamed. The bald man felt the shiny surface of his head and gasped. The doorman lurched towards Lara and she threw the hairy frisbee at him, right in his face. The doorman brought the chair smashing down, missing Lara but demolishing the bald man's table. Lara was away. She knew the front door was closed so she ran for an open window. It was going to be a tight squeeze but she went for it anyway, leaping through the gap and out on to the pavement.

The Cook kids had been pressed up against the locked door of the hotel, trying to see what was happening inside. When Lara bounded up to them they smothered her with kisses and hugs.

Get off me, she shrugged. Lara was a Spy Dog again, her bullet–holed ear standing taller than ever. *I'm after some baddies. A young bloke, running like mad. And a lady with a large nose. Which way?* she panted. *Oh, if only I could talk*, she howled.

Ben pointed to a man sprinting round the corner. 'Is that who you're chasing, Lara?' he asked. 'And it looks like the professor too.' *It most certainly is*, barked Lara. *You have got a superbrain, Ben! Come on, guys, let's get them.*

Christopher Bent was full of energy, spurred on by the prospect of selling the brain formula for millions. Dame Payne clopped along in her heels but it was the professor whose lungs were soon heaving.

He stopped and clutched his chest. 'I can't run any more,' he puffed, bending double to recover. The professor raised his head and saw Lara and the children bounding round the corner. 'Oh no,' he gasped. 'The kids. I can't have them following me.' Lara and the children saw the professor up ahead and stopped in their tracks. Professor Cortex fixed Lara with an icy stare that sent a shiver down her spine. 'Sorry, GM451,' he shouted. 'But you must stop following us. Your priority has to be the children. Keep them safe.'

Lara watched as he hailed a taxi and the three escapees bundled in. *Perhaps the man was right after all*, thought Lara. *I still can't believe it but the professor seems to have turned bad.*

Ben, Ollie and Sophie caught up with Lara. 'I'm sure that woman is my head teacher, Dame Payne,' said Ben, catching his breath. 'Maybe she's been kidnapped too! What can we do, Lara?' he asked. 'They've all disappeared, and why did the professor get into the taxi with them?'

Why indeed? shrugged Lara, her brain whirring. The dog raised her paw and hailed the next taxi. The driver pulled up and watched with a confused frown as they piled in. 'Where to, kids?' he asked.

Ben looked at Lara. *Go on, lad*, she willed. *I know you've always wanted to say it.*

Ben shrugged. 'Er, follow that cab?' he

asked, pointing to the professor's taxi some distance ahead.

Christopher Bent had a tight hold on the professor's laptop. His plan was to take some of the brain potion at the earliest opportunity, then log on to the professor's laptop, learn the secret and make sure he remained permanently brainy. Then he would either set up an Internet site to sell the potion worldwide or make a living from game shows. He wasn't sure which yet, but either way he would be rich beyond his wildest dreams.

Dame Payne had similar thoughts whirring through her mind. Neither planned on sharing. They exchanged cold smiles in the taxi, each scheming to double-cross the other.

Lara and the children watched from a distance as Dame Payne, Christopher Bent and the professor queued for rail tickets. Lara couldn't help thinking the professor looked extremely nervous. She was racking her brain to come up with an innocent explanation. *Why on earth is the professor getting on the train with these evil people?* she wondered. *And why did he run away when he saw us? It doesn't look good. I suppose it's no wonder he's looking so edgy.* She considered what to do next. As she saw it, they didn't have many options and she wasn't keen on getting the children into any more danger. She cringed as she thought about what Mum would say. *At least the trio don't know we're following them*, she thought. *They think they're home and dry. All we have to do is find a way on to their train and I'm sure a plan will follow.*

Bent and the professor left the ticket counter and strolled towards platform six. Lara pushed Ben forward and he approached the ticket office. He began badly. 'Er . . . Can I have some tickets on the same train as those three people who were just here?' he asked.

'To London?' asked the ticket lady.

'Yes, please.' Ben smiled. 'Three children and a dog.'

The lady eyed Ben suspiciously. 'Three kids and a dog?' she questioned. 'Shouldn't you children be with an adult?' The ticket lady poked her head out of the kiosk and looked at Sophie, Ollie and Lara. Ollie waved. Sophie looked down at her shoes.

Lara cringed. *Just give us the tickets, lady*, she urged.

'Where's your mum?' quizzed the lady. 'And you must put your dog on a lead.'

'Oh, forget it,' said Ben. 'You're right, the train isn't for us.' He turned away with Sophie, Ollie and Lara and stared up at the departure board.

The ticket lady was still watching them, so Sophie took Lara's lead out of her pocket and clipped it on to her collar.

'We've got exactly three minutes before the London train on platform six departs,' explained Ben. 'But we haven't got any tickets. Let's go to the platform and see if we can find a way to sneak on.'

Great, thought Lara, bounding alongside the children as they rushed across the station. *Just the kind of thing I used to do when I was a secret agent!*

'Quick,' said Sophie excitedly, 'there's no one at the ticket barrier.'

The children raced towards the platform and through the gates, just as the guard's whistle blew.

Hurry, kids, Lara woofed. *That's the signal for the train to leave and we're not on it yet.*

Ben grabbed Ollie's hand and they all sprinted for the train, just making it on board as the doors beeped and closed behind them. Within seconds the children and their pet were away, speeding towards London.

16. Tickets, Please?

Ben, Sophie, Ollie and Lara stood in the cramped corridor of the train as it pulled out of the station. 'What now?' asked Ollie.

'Not sure,' replied Ben. 'I suppose we have to find the baddies and let Lara loose on them. Hopefully, she'll know what to do.'

Lara gave an excited woof as Sophie bent down and unclipped her lead. *I can't wait to find them and save the professor*, she thought.

They were standing in the swaying part of the train, between carriages. Lara looked at the kids, their encouraging eyes gazing at her. *What? You expect me to come up with a plan? I'd better get my Spy Dog head on. A plan, Lara. A cunning plan. What should we do first?* she thought, strumming her paw against the carriage floor. She spied the ticket collector coming down the carriage. *Yikes. Part one of the plan is to avoid him.* Lara stood and jabbed her paw in the direction of the ticket collector.

Ben and Sophie looked panicky. 'What if he throws us off the train?' exclaimed Sophie.

'He might know where the baddies are sitting,' offered Ollie. 'Maybe he would help us.'

Lara took two seconds to consider the situation. She ran through Ollie's suggestion in her head. She pictured Ben explaining that there was a pair of criminals and a mad professor somewhere on the train. And they were stealing a top-secret brain formula that was going to make millions. And that the children and their dog were going to solve the crime. And that their dog was in fact a highly trained secret agent. *Mmm,* she thought, *on an unbelievability scale of 1 to 10, it's an 11. He's going to throw us straight off the train.* She looked at the corridor. *Quickly,* she beckoned. *Let's hide in the loo.*

Lara pressed the button and the toilet door swished open. They all crammed into the tiny train toilet and the door swished shut. Sophie pressed the lock. Ben sat on the toilet seat with Ollie on his knee while Sophie and Lara squeezed up against the sink, hardly able to breathe. And all of them stopped breathing completely when they heard the ticket collector knock on the door.

'Tickets, please,' he yelled. 'Whoever's in there, I need to see your tickets.'

'We haven't got tickets,' mouthed Sophie to Lara.

'I need a wee,' whispered Ollie to his big brother.

'Hang on just a minute,' shouted Ben. 'I'm, er, just finishing.' He looked at Lara. 'What do we do now?' he mouthed. 'He's waiting for us.'

Let him wait a bit, thought Lara, waving her paws up and down to calm the children. *I need to escape. And there seems only one way out.* Lara stood and pointed to the small skylight. *Can someone help me open this, please?*

'No way, Lara,' whispered Sophie. 'This train is going at a hundred miles an hour. You'll be killed.'

Lara shrugged. *It's not ideal*, she thought.

But if the ticket inspector catches me he'll throw us off at the next station and we'll never get to the bottom of this mystery. The roof's the only hiding place.

Sophie took Ollie as Ben stood on the toilet seat and pulled the skylight open. A whooshing noise filled the tiny bathroom. Ben gave Lara a leg up and she poked her head out of the top of the carriage. She looked forward, her eyes squinting into the wind, her ears blown flat against her head as the trees flashed by. *This is definitely a fast train*, she agreed. Lara looked backwards, across the top of the snaking carriages, fur and ears obscuring her view. Finally she looked back down at the children. *It is difficult*, she decided. *But with a bit of a push I may be able to make it up there.*

There was another knock at the door, this time more urgent. 'Come on,' bellowed the ticket inspector. 'I haven't got all day.'

OK, that's the decision made, thought Lara. She positioned her back paws on Ben's shoulders and scrambled upwards. *Ouch, it's a tight squeeze.* Ben stood carefully, his pet's claws digging into his shoulders.

'Careful, girl,' he whispered as her back legs wobbled. He pushed her legs up and watched as she scrabbled to get a grip on the roof. Sophie and Ollie held their hands over their mouths as they watched Lara's legs disappear. Within a few seconds she was gone and Ben closed the skylight before climbing down off the toilet seat. He gave a silent thumbs-up.

The children looked at each other and nodded. 'Let's do it,' whispered Ben, filling his chest with a deep breath. Sophie pressed the button to flush the toilet. Ollie pressed the lock and the toilet door swung open. The ticket collector was frowning beneath his peaked cap.

Ollie smiled his very best smile. 'I was desperate,' he explained. 'In fact we all were. We always go together,' he explained. His elder brother and sister nodded enthusiastically.

'Can I see your tickets, please?' reminded the inspector.

'Of course,' said Ben, taking over. 'My dad's got them.'

'And where's he?' asked the ticket collector suspiciously.

'Can't quite remember which way we came,' said Ben, doing his best puzzled expression. 'He's quite an old chap. Nearly bald. Three white hairs combed over the top. Have you seen him?'

The ticket collector nodded. 'He's sitting with a man and a woman, in first class,' he said, pointing a helpful finger towards the front of the train. 'I'll be back to check your tickets in a few minutes, OK?'

The children gave their friendliest smiles and started to sway their way towards the front of the train.

On top of the train, Lara gripped the roof with all her might. Her ears flapped wildly and her eyes were watering. The skylight was closed so there was no going back. Luckily, each carriage had three skylights so she had something to wind her paws round and hang on to. She lay for a minute, squinting into the gale, thinking about her next move. *One wrong move and I'm a gonner.* Lara decided the best thing to do would be to move along the train, peering into the skylights. *Maybe I'll spot the professor,* she thought. *But first I need*

to make it to the next skylight without being blown away!

She slithered, snake-like, across the roof of the train carriage, her eyes squinting in the hurricane-force gale. *I can hardly catch my breath.* A train hurtled past in the opposite direction, scaring her half to death. Her train was now running alongside a motorway and she caught the eye of a lorry driver. *I'm just getting some fresh air!* she yapped. The driver shook his head, and Lara watched his truck indicate left as he turned into the next service station in search of some strong coffee.

Lara edged her way to the next skylight and peered down at the passengers. *No professor. Move on.* She reached the end of the carriage and peered down, hoping to see a door that she could slip through. *Nothing. Doh. I'll have to jump to the next carriage*, she thought.

Lara practised standing up, gingerly at first, the wind almost blowing her off her feet. She stayed crouched on all fours, then raised her head to check there were no tunnels. *That would be a disaster*, she thought. The track stretched ahead in a perfect line, coming together at the horizon. *OK, here goes*, she nodded, taking as deep a breath as she could. Then she pulled back on her hind legs and sprang, cat-like, crossing the divide and scrambling for a hold on the next carriage. *Yes!* she howled into the wind. *I did it.*

She looked at the train snaking into the distance and counted in her head. *Five more carriages to go*, she considered. *One of them must have a way in. Oh, please let there be a way in.* Lara pondered the children down below, probably captured by the ticket collector. *Or, even worse, captured by the villains. I have to keep moving.* She lay down in the roaring wind and began another slow belly crawl down the carriage.

17. First-class Spying

The children made their way through four carriages, looking out for the professor all the time. Ben looked round at his sister and brother. He pointed to the sign on the next carriage. 'First class,' he said. 'This is where it could get interesting.'

They pressed the button and the door to first class swished open. The carriage was almost empty. Ben, Sophie and Ollie walked slowly down the aisle, past a few people typing on laptops or snoozing. There were three people sitting at the far end, deep in conversation. Ben recognized the back of the professor's shiny head. Dame Payne and a younger man were facing them, so Ben pretended to look at something on the floor as they sank into the seats behind the professor. Quiet as mice, they listened.

Ben heard the professor talking about his formula. 'It's instant genius,' he explained. 'But it's for animals. It's really not safe for humans.'

'I've already tried it, remember?' said the young man. 'And it does work. Do we have a deal, Professor?'

The scientist thought through the 'deal'. There didn't seem to be any option if he wanted to save Ben's life. 'We have a deal, Bent,' mumbled the professor. 'I will produce the formula for you, but then I want out. I will not be involved in putting children in danger.'

Ben couldn't believe his ears. 'Surely not,' he whispered. 'The professor can't be a baddie. He can't be selling his top-secret formula. And why are children in danger? That must be why Dame Payne is here.'

'This is my retirement fund,' said Dame Payne. 'The people I have been working with will not be happy that I'm double-crossing them.' Ben shuddered at the sound of his head teacher's voice. He'd always thought she was evil, and here was the proof.

The startled children listened closely until the conversation finished. 'I need a coffee,' sighed Dame Payne, standing up and grabbing her handbag.

Ben tried to duck down but it was too late. She nodded at Sophie and Ollie and did a double take at Ben. He put on an innocent smile. 'Hi, Miss,' he cringed.

'Mr Benjamin Cook!' exclaimed the sinister head teacher. 'My star pupil. What a coincidence. Tell me, what exactly are you doing on this train?'

The professor's head peered over the seat. 'Ben and Sophie,' he exclaimed. 'And Oliver. What? How? Where . . .?' he began.

'Friends of yours, Professor Cortex?' asked Dame Payne, raising her eyebrow.

'Well, yes,' stammered the professor. 'Sort of.' He looked around anxiously, presumably for GM451, expecting her to come out of hiding. 'Look here, children,' he said. 'I don't know why you're on this train or how you got here, but I'm in the middle of something rather urgent. It's a bit dangerous actually, especially for you, Ben. It's best you leave.'

'We heard you talking, Professor,' challenged Ben. 'We know what you're up to. We heard everything. I can't believe you'd sell out to this pair of dimwits,' he babbled, pointing at Dame Payne and Christopher Bent. 'I mean, how could you?' yelled Ben, tears rising in his voice.

'You don't know what you're talking about, Benjamin,' warned the professor. 'I'm here because I've finally invented something that's worth a fortune and these people are offering me a deal.' He glared at Ben. 'It's an especially good deal for you!' he hissed under his breath. 'Please leave now, before you get into big trouble.'

'Too late for that,' growled Ben's head teacher, reaching into her handbag and pulling out a pistol. 'Sit down, nutty professor. And you horrible lot can come and sit closer, where I can keep an eye on you. Now I have the formula *and* the perfect young brain. I love it when a plan falls into place.' She pushed the children into seats next to Professor Cortex, waving her pistol in a menacing way. 'I don't quite know what's going on, but I have a sneaky feeling you're trying to trick me. Any funny business and someone will get hurt. Am I understood?'

The children nodded down the barrel of the gun. Things had never been clearer.

Lara had battled her way through the howling wind. She'd slithered across four carriages, and jumped the gaps, finally arriving on top of first class. She was able to stare down on the luxury seats below, and no one had

noticed a wild-eared dog peering through the ceiling portholes. But Lara had seen the professor's ping-pong-ball head. She'd spied it from above and had been concerned to see the children sneak into the seats behind — then alarmed when they'd been discovered . . . and beside herself when the woman had pulled a gun.

Uh-oh, she thought. *Nightmare scenario. Again!* Lara considered her options, which seemed very limited. The children were now in grave danger so her priority switched from catching baddies to rescuing her family. There was only one way in.

She gathered her thoughts, still clinging on for dear life. From nowhere another high-speed train thundered by, jolting Lara and causing her to let go of the skylight. The gale caught her and she slid alarmingly across the roof, on her furry tummy, trying to stop herself by jabbing her claws into the paint-work. Her nails screeched like chalk on a blackboard as she dug as deep as she could. She caught the last remaining skylight and pulled with her paws and teeth, steadying herself as her back legs flew behind her. *Hold tight, Lara,* she urged herself, the wind filling her cheeks and puffing them out like a bullfrog. *Let go and you're an ex-Spy Dog.* The train was still rattling at full speed but Lara had to get back to the skylight above the children. *I have to attempt a rescue*, she thought, sliding herself back along the carriage.

Lara looked below and saw the children. She raised her head to check all around. Her heart sank. *Just when I thought it couldn't get any worse*, she thought. *There's a tunnel up ahead.* Lara calculated that she had about two minutes before the train entered the tunnel. She didn't like the look of the black hole ahead — railway tunnels were narrow and low. *Just enough room for a train*, she imagined. *But maybe not enough to squeeze a dog through too. I have to work quickly. No time for thinking. Just do something. Now!*

18. Tunnel Vision

Lara glanced up at the tunnel, which was getting bigger every second. *No, I didn't imagine it.* The skylight was her only chance. *It's the only way in*, she panicked, *and it's the only way I'm going to save my skin.*

Lara lay flat, held on with her three paws and felt for the button on her collar with the fourth. She pressed the catch and caught the mini-screwdriver, then watched as her collar blew away into the distance. Then she fixed the handle of the tool between her teeth and attacked the first screw. She twisted her mouth. Then again. And again, until the screw came away. *Three more to go*, she thought, glancing up at the looming black hole. The train sped on as Lara wrestled with the second and third screws. Her mouth was aching. *One final screw*, she thought. *Stay calm, girl*, she willed, glancing up at the blackness, now only thirty seconds away. *It looks awfully tight. Maybe if I just lie flat I will survive*, she thought. She looked again. *It hardly looks tall enough for a train to get through, never mind an upstairs passenger!*

Lara worked the last screw loose and spat out the screwdriver. The dog was a tiny dot against the massive rock face. The driver sounded his horn as his train thundered towards the darkness. She had no time to think as she put her claws under the rim and levered off the skylight. The Spy Dog fell headlong through the hole, just as the train entered the tunnel.

The first-class passengers heard a whoosh of wind and looked up to see a black and white dog falling from the heavens. They watched as she landed in a crumpled heap, quickly righting herself and standing tall, in a martial arts position. Lara looked as menacing as she could, curling her lip and raising her hackles at the lady with the gun. *I've met your sort before*, she snarled. *Now let the children go.*

'Lara!' squealed Sophie. 'You're alive.'

'GM451,' exclaimed the professor. 'What on earth are you doing?'

What does it look like, Prof? snarled the Spy Dog. *You trained me and now it looks like you've betrayed us all. How could you do it?*

Dame Payne looked at Lara's curled lip and stepped back.

'She's a superdog,' warned the professor. 'You're finished now. She's a karate black belt.'

Dame Payne recognized Lara's picture from one of the staff meetings. 'She won't be so super when she gets a bullet in her,' she threatened. She turned the gun on the snarling dog and tightened her finger on the trigger. 'Your superdog will be a dead dog.'

'No, please,' cried the professor. 'GM451 is my greatest achievement. She's my life. I won't do a thing for you if you hurt her!'

The head teacher glanced sideways at the professor, while keeping the pistol trained on the dangerous dog. 'Well,' she spat, 'all life has to come to an end.'

The children and the professor watched as Dame Payne turned back to their beloved dog. They saw the desperation in Lara's eyes. *What can I do?* she thought. *Leap at her and I'm dead. Stand here and I'm dead. How am I going to save the children?*

One of the other passengers pulled the emergency cord as Dame Payne squeezed the trigger. The train screeched to a halt, throwing the passengers everywhere. Professor Cortex was already in mid-air, leaping to protect Lara. The shot rang out and the passengers bolted under their seats. The professor lay in a crumpled heap, in front of the dog he'd tried to protect. Dame Payne didn't blink. She pointed the pistol at the Spy Dog and pulled the trigger again.

Nothing, except a click. And another click. And a third. Dame Payne cursed. She threw her gun to the ground and ran for the exit, but Lara already had the teacher in her sights. She brought the woman crashing to the ground and sank her teeth into a bony ankle. Lara took a firm hold and growled. Dame Payne screamed. She crawled along the floor, Lara hanging on to her foot. She made it as far as the toilet and forced the door open. Then she managed to shake Lara off and quickly hit the 'door close' button. 'Keep away from me, dog,' she yelled.

Ben charged up and stood alongside Lara. 'If you take one step outside, I'll set our Spy Dog on you,' he warned. 'She'll be here waiting.' Lara bounded back into the first-class carriage where passengers were frantically dialling the police on their mobile phones. She turned to the professor, who was still sprawled across the seats. There was a hole in his jacket. It was perfectly round, like the one in her ear. Blood was seeping out. Sophie was sobbing and holding his hand.

Christopher Bent was frozen with fear. Ollie was warning him not to move or his dog would karate chop him. But it didn't look as though Bent could even twitch his eye; he was so scared. Lara put her paw to the professor's cheek. *He's so cold*, she shivered. His eyes opened halfway.

'GM451?' he whispered. 'You're OK. I'm so proud of you.'

Hang on in there, Prof, she willed. *The ambulance will be here in a tick. Keep talking, old fella.*

The professor's eyes had closed and his

voice was distant. 'It's not what it seems,' he gasped. 'Please don't remember me like this.' The professor opened his eyes a little and managed a half smile. Blood trickled from the corner of his mouth and his chest rattled. 'I'm not only proud of you, Lara,' he murmured. 'I love you too.'

Lara nuzzled the old man's forehead and planted a lick on his cheek. She looked frantically round at the children. 'Is he going to be OK?' wept Sophie. 'I mean, he's bleeding and everything.'

Lara looked back at the professor. His eyes were closed and his face had turned grey. *It's not looking great*, she thought. *We need a doctor, quick.* Lara felt the professor's body go limp.

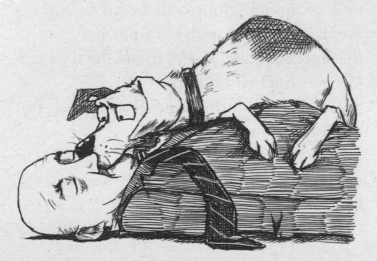

Suddenly policemen swarmed into the first-class carriage. Christopher Bent was dragged away. Dame Payne was shouting from the toilet and threatening to kill everyone, so armed police carefully opened the door and she was soon led away in cuffs.

The children and Lara were hurried away and wrapped in foil blankets. They watched through misty eyes as the professor was stretchered into a waiting ambulance.

'This is so awful,' cried Sophie.

'Poor Professor,' wept Ollie.

'He saved Lara's life,' stammered Ben.

And he called me Lara, howled GM451.

19. Weird Science

The children sat at the front of the church, scrubbed and cleaned. Mum had taken charge of Ben's hair, combing it in a side parting. He'd fought and lost. As a result, he sat next to his brother and sister, looking subdued, praying his friends wouldn't see him. Mum and Dad sat in one of the middle rows, proud of their beautiful children. Lara was sitting in the front pew. While the children sang their hearts out, Lara barked along to the hymns as best she could. 'The Lord's my shepherd, I'll not want . . .' she howled. The children sat on the hard bench, listening to the vicar droning on and on. Ollie struggled to stay interested.

Finally, the ceremony was over and Ben

craned his neck to catch Dad's eye. Dad nodded and that was the signal for Lara and the children to make their escape through the back door of the church. Ben tore off his tie and messed up his hair, delighted to be free. 'This way,' he yelled. 'He'll be waiting for us round the front.'

Their faces lit up as they saw the old man in the wheelchair. Ben was there first, throwing his arms round Professor Cortex. 'Oh, we're so glad to see you,' yelled Ben. 'And we're so relieved that you're all right. You've been in hospital for ages.'

'I will be in hospital again if you squeeze me that tightly, young man,' joked the professor, feeling the wound in his shoulder. 'It still hurts, I can tell you. How did the christening go?'

'Boring,' sang Ollie. 'The vicar put some water on the baby's head and she just screamed the place down.'

'How long will you be in the wheelchair, Professor?' asked Sophie.

'I'm making good progress,' said the old man. 'Not too long, I hope.'

'We never *really* believed you'd turned

bad,' admitted Ben. 'We knew there'd be a logical explanation.'

The professor looked at Lara, who was wagging enthusiastically. 'I think GM451 had her doubts,' he replied, grinning. 'It must have looked a bit strange, especially when you heard me talking to those evil people on the train.'

Just a bit, thought Lara. *I didn't want to believe it but it sure looked fishy.*

'But I had to go along with them, you see, because I needed to protect Ben. That was the only deal I did. To think, Benjamin, they wanted your brain on a plate!'

Ben grimaced and ruffled his hair, reassuring himself that his head was still attached. 'They were going to use my brain in their formula. How gruesome. I hope Dame Payne stays behind bars for a long time.'

'She's plain old "Miss Payne" again,' the professor reminded him.

'Did they catch Mr Wilde?' asked Ben.

'He was still tied to his chair,' laughed Professor Cortex. 'He and the other teachers will be severely punished.'

'And what about Christopher Bent?' asked

Sophie. 'He's dead rich. He won a million pounds on *Who Wants to Be a Millionaire?*, although I guess it was your formula that helped him, Professor.'

'Ah, yes. Not exactly Employee of the Month,' the professor admitted. Then he smiled. 'There's an old saying,' he added, 'that a fool and his money are easily parted.'

'What does that mean?' asked Ollie.

'Basically, Mr Oliver, it means that Christopher Bent is back to being as stupid as he was before. He's already gambled his fortune away. He will be spending the next few years in prison.'

'I'm so glad Dame Payne is behind bars,' sighed Ben. 'She was horrible. Do you really think she would have used my brain? I wonder who we'll get to replace her? We'll need loads of new teachers now.'

'Oh, I don't know about the new head teacher,' said the professor, smiling, 'but I've heard a rumour about your new head of science. Starts on Monday, apparently.'

'Who?' asked Sophie, her eyes sparkling.

Professor Cortex couldn't control his grin. 'Who do you think?'

'No way!' yelled Ben.

'Absolutely,' beamed the professor. 'I've always wanted to teach. It turns out that my brain formula does work on humans, but only for a while. It needs tweaking otherwise we only get temporary geniuses. And that'll never do. Wouldn't it be good if we could work on it during science lessons?' The professor's eyes were alive at the thought of having so many willing helpers. 'And I won't be needing any brains as ingredients,' he added, raising his eyebrow at Ben. 'But the real reason is that your mum says she wants to keep me where she can see me. She says she doesn't want any more dangerous scrapes and reckons we'll all be safer if I steer clear of Spy School.' The old man looked round at the children, whose faces were filled with delight. He winked at them. 'Not sure I can promise to stay away completely, but I'll certainly be keeping busy at my new school!'

Ben, Sophie and Ollie grinned at each other before all eyes rested on Lara. The family pet sat upright and puffed out her chest. She knew her odd ears looked a bit foolish, especially the one with the hole. But

Lara was proud of her bullet hole. She was proud that the professor now had one too, because he cared about her. *He called me Lara*, she reminded herself. *I'm a family pet first*, she wagged. *But a Spy Dog second. If adventure comes calling then what's a dog supposed to do?*